The Wulfenite Affair & Other Stories

Also by S.K.Johannesen

Sister Patsy

Luggas Wood

The Yellow Room

The Wulfenite Affair

& Other Stories

S.K. Johannesen

efp

the electric ferry press / kitchener

Copyright © 2012, S.K.Johannesen

All rights reserved. No part of this text may be reproduced or transmitted in any form or by any means, electronic or mechanical, or by any information storage and retrieval system, without express written permission of the publisher.

Published in Canada by The Electric Ferry Press

Library and Archives Canada
Cataloguing in Publication

Johannesen, Stanley
The Wulfenite affair and other stories / S.K.Johannesen.

Short stories.
ISBN 978-0-9881098-1-0

I. Title.
PS8569.O266W84 2012   C813'.6   C2012-904347-8

Portions of this work have appeared in *Grain*, *The Malahat Review*, *Of(f)course*, and *Queen's Quarterly*.

Cover drawing by the author.

Table of Contents

The Wulfenite Affair	1
Brother Bringsrud	60
Solveig	74
Old Photos	88
Brückenkopfstrasse	99
Réfléchissez	109
The Artist of the Prayer Room	118
Pont Neuf	133
Venus on the Malecón	155
Prodigal Returns	164
The Walk	174
Afterword	180

The Wulfenite Affair

1

I felt from the first, when he told me the story of Pra and Sylvia, José and J.B., Daniel and Tamayo, that there was something morbidly self-regarding in it—as though he were the only person in the world with an uncomfortable secret. Since his death, however, the irritation has abated, and I find myself increasingly drawn to the weird beauty of his story of love and betrayal, to the peculiar psychology of its protagonist and, not least, to its elusive heroine, the girl, Sylvia.

How I came to know Octavius is not important. The events to be recounted here took place long before we met.

Octavius had been abandoned when a child. His Italian mother, married in 1940 to an aging Norwegian bachelor named Ragnar Sivertsen, died the next year giving birth to Octavius. His father disappeared. Octavius eventually learned that he had died in Baltimore, a skid-row derelict. By this time Octavius had already changed his surname from Sivertsen to Stevens.

Octavius was handed around among members of the Pentecostal sect his parents had belonged to in the Sunset Park district of Brooklyn, and at fourteen ran away from an elderly couple who were well-intentioned but wholly unsuitable guardians. I understood only so much. He spoke very little of his childhood. Yet I have no trouble imagining the young Octavius. He could not have been altogether a child, just as he was not, later, altogether a grown man. These traits—the residue of an eerie precocity with the retarded social development of the adult—might have made him an unappealing friend, but it was in fact, and not by any means to me alone, his most arresting quality. He was successful in attracting the love of women, although these affairs inevitably ended badly. Octavius was aware of the devastation he left behind in his relations with women. It fed his morbidity, as well as his vanity, without leading to any insight that might prevent such disasters from repeating themselves.

Octavius first broached the subject one evening about two years before he died. He arrived at my door without warning and in a sombre mood. He was evidently deeply disturbed by something. I fixed him a whisky and water and waited for him to say what had brought him.

I should say that these visits had become rarer over the years. Not because our interests had diverged, or because we had grown tired of one another's company. The truth is there were often great distances separating us. He spent years at a time abroad. Something in banking. My business likewise took me away for lengths of time. We were both drawn to Europe, although we never met there. He was drawn to the South and to all things Mediterranean, as I was drawn to all things Northern and Atlantic. This difference in taste extended to food and drink, music, art, favourite cities, literature, films. Far from driving us apart, it became the subject-matter, more often the sub-text, of our deepest exchanges, on life and art, religion and human destiny. We wrote letters. I have file-boxes of his letters. I know he kept mine. In these letters we were much more candid with one another than we could have been in person. Nor did our friendship suffer from the sometimes long gaps between our exchanges. In very nearly the last letter I sent him I remarked on this capacity we had to pick up the thread of conversation after these lapses. I joked that I expected one of us would learn one day about the death of the other only after his funeral—from the return, perhaps, of an undelivered letter. I said perhaps that would be the best way. In the event, that is more or less how it was.

He told me the story I have come to think of as the wulfenite affair at intervals over a period of some months following his first visit. I encouraged his telling. I did not contradict him or quiz him about anything he said, other than to get him to clarify obscure parts of the narrative. He died without giving me another opportunity to pursue it with him. And so, in a way, this account is my response to him. If I appear to embellish here and there, it is to bring out what I feel was implicit in what he said, or to connect things he told out of sequence. I think I do not do violence to his sense of the facts or what he meant by telling them. None of it can matter to him now.

2

Octavius had learned, later than most people, that information might be got on the internet, and that one thing might lead to another. In the course of other work he would sometimes, he said, type into the search engine the words Hope Mine, and sometimes Amado.

Amado was a place in Arizona, little more than a filling station, motel and bar with an artificial duck pond and a few willow trees. An oasis of sorts. I have never been there, or to anywhere else in the Arizona desert. But from Octavius's description, and by studying the topographical map of the district, I have no trouble imagining it. Over the highway from this resort, behind a line of poor bungalows and shanties shimmering in the heat off the asphalt, stood a railroad siding and an unroofed loading platform on the Santa Fe track between Tucson and Nogales. That was Amado. An utterly insignificant place. Nevertheless, it turned up on tourist web sites as a starting point for treks into the Santa Rita mountains to the east. One of the places you could get to from Amado was the Hope Mine, an abandoned lead and silver mine where the events I am about to relate took place, more than fifty years ago now as I write this.

For a time Octavius found only incidental references to the mine in geological reports and soil surveys. Once, there was an announcement that the entrance had been bulldozed over by the Park Service for safety reasons—there were many such old mines dotting the hillsides, with concealed shafts and tunnels treacherous with rotting timbers. Later there was an announcement that a mining company were going to re-open the Hope Mine. Their plan was to use the latest methods to locate valuable mineral specimens overlooked in earlier operations.

The mineral they hoped to find, Octavius explained, was wulfenite, a crystalline form of lead ore, an oxide of lead and molybdenum, named for the eighteenth-century Austrian Jesuit, Franz Xaver Freiherr von Wulfen, who first described it in field notes on the natural history of his native Carinthia. This same von Wulfen, I learned, is memorialized in the purple-flowering evergreen plant, *Wulfenia carinthiaca*, found, it is said, only on two mountains in the Carinthian Alps. Wulfenite, on the other hand, has been found in many other places around the world, not least in the played-out lead and silver mines of southern Arizona and the neighbouring Mexican states of Sonora and Chihuahua.

Octavius made discreet enquiries and found, to his relief, that the plan to re-open the Hope Mine had come to nothing.

Then Octavius saw the story, buried in a report of local news in the on-line files of a Tucson newspaper. Octavius had printed the page and marked the item with heavy vertical lines in both margins. It was dated about ten months earlier than his visit to me. Either his search had failed to catch it before now, or the material had only recently been posted.

There had been a disturbance at the university museum in Tucson. A visitor, during public visiting hours, had been expelled after an altercation, first with the museum guards and then with a staff curator. The man, unnamed in the article, was judged to be in his seventies, medium height, athletic build, dressed in worn denims and cowboy boots, and was heard by witnesses to say that wulfenite specimens on display in the mineral collections of the museum had been stolen from him. He demanded the specimens be returned. There was a scuffle. The news item concluded by saying that no charges were laid in the incident, and that the museum declined to comment other than to say there was no basis for anything in the man's story. The specimens were from various places in Arizona and Mexico. All had been in the collections of the university museum for at least forty years.

I read this over two or three times, as much to give myself time to gauge Octavius's state of mind as to take in the details of the report, which meant nothing to me. I asked him if he had followed this up. Octavius said he had managed to get the phone number of the reporter and speak with him, and the reporter told Octavius he knew little more than what he had written. He remembered the man claiming that someone at the university had got these specimens from him by pretending to borrow them for study purposes and had then sold them on to the museum as his own. The reporter thought he had better not put this in the printed story. The guards and other witnesses he interviewed did not think the man was demented. He seemed educated and, although roughly dressed, had about him an air of self-assurance and perhaps even of money. A man plainly used to getting his way, they said. They did not know who he was and had never seen him before. He had not so far turned up again.

"You know who it was," I said, anticipating him.

Octavius did not respond at once. He took a sip of whisky and leaned back in his chair, his eyes far away. The initial tension had drained out of him. His eyes gradually focused on a picture hanging on my wall. A modern Japanese print. One of my treasures. Moonlight on a calm sea, and a boat, from the bow of which hangs a small lantern casting a yellow circle of light on the inky water. A man is spear-fishing.

"I know exactly who it was," he said.

3

The first time Octavius saw Sylvia, he said, she was sitting in Pra's pickup. Just sitting, not getting out, or making to get out. The truck was white. Her hair was black. An oval face, an olive Mexican face, framed by black hair. He saw her from a distance, from over by the derelict cabins on the south side of the arroyo. The white pickup, with the girl in it, sat in the middle of a flat empty space, where the dump trucks turned around when they came to load up from the ore hopper. Across this space and overlooking it lay the main camp building. The chief miner, Tamayo, a lean dry Indian of uncertain age, and Daniel, his burly assistant, slept in one of the two rooms. The other room served as a general gathering place and cookhouse where Octavius made their beans and tortillas on a propane cook stove. Behind the building was the mine entrance, an insignificant black hole from which issued a narrow-gauge track that forked one way to the great pile of tailings and the other way to the red metal ore hopper.

Octavius stared at the girl with a self-defeating intensity, trying to bring detail into focus in the glare of mid-day and across too great a distance. Who could be sitting there in Pra's truck? He never doubted this visitation was about him, somehow. And why was she sitting like that? Sitting away from the window, not hanging an elbow out like American girls, or showing any impatience or petulance. Was she hot, or thirsty? She showed no curiosity in her surroundings. She did not crane her neck or lean forward. Octavius could not make out whether her eyes were turned in his direction. They might be or might not be. Maybe she had already picked him out, although he was perfectly still and partly concealed. Mexicans saw things other people would miss. They disliked jerky movements, or anything that was not economical and spare. And so he didn't move anything, not even to shift his weight.

The over-bright scene burned itself into memory as he waited. The white pickup with the girl in the wide alkali expanse in the centre of the circle made by turning ore trucks. The red metal ore hopper. The long ridge of tailings extending out from the small black hole in the mountain. The white, tin-roofed cabin. Still the girl did not move.

Abruptly, knowing by instinct that if she had seen him this would be the right thing to do, Octavius turned away and walked rapidly in the other direction. Over the desert scrub, down and up across dry stream beds that scored the desert floor, in a straight line about a mile to the south, to a place he could find unerringly, having been here many times before. An old filled-in digging, the metal skeleton of a Model A car, chewed grey mine timbers and sheets of corrugated iron scattered about, and the four cinder-block walls of a roofless shed. From a hole down low on the inside of one of the walls, Octavius retrieved the remnants of a Mexican comic-strip novel he kept hidden there. He reclined on a rough plank bench in the centre of this sanctuary and opened the tattered book to his favourite place.

4

The soda biscuits and the flour tortillas started the same way. Flour and baking soda sifted onto the oil-cloth-covered table through a piece of wire screen nailed to a wooden frame. Melted lard and sour milk poured a little at a time into a well in the centre of the mound of flour, and all this worked into dough, sticky and lumpy for the biscuits, floury and smooth for the tortillas.

Twice a week Octavius picked over the pinto beans and put them to soak in one of two enamelled pots. While the beans soaked in one, the other held already-cooked beans, reheated twice a day, adding meat from time to time. Salt pork, or deer or javelina when Pra had shot something. Sometimes just the beans, mashed in a skillet with fat and eaten scooped up in a flour tortilla. Always the succulent green jalapeño peppers.

Daniel and Tamayo complained about the food. Octavius liked the monotony of it, the subtle shift in the taste of the bean pot from day to day, the fiery contrast of the peppers, his routine with the biscuits and the tortillas. The biscuits they ate in the morning, with coffee and rancid butter, and honey. José found the honey.

José walked out of the desert one day. From the south, all the way from Durango, he said. Certainly the thirty miles or so from Nogales. He never asked about pay or hours, or even about a job. He started doing things. Neat in his person, with a sparse untrimmed beard, José observed everything with the same sweet and ironical disinterest. He seemed to know about mining, and so fitted in with Daniel and Tamayo, with the drilling and blasting and timbering at the work face, while Octavius and J.B. shovelled ore and worked the winch, and pushed the ore cars through the tunnels on the narrow-gauge tracks. Pra himself never worked underground.

The day they got the honey, José climbed up the hill just above the mine entrance, to a patch of flowering cactus plants. He lay on the ground alongside this thicket, studying something in the air above his head. Occasionally he lifted himself on one elbow and squinted in the direction of the ridge high above. Once he shifted position entirely, moving to another cactus patch, where he repeated the procedure.

When he was satisfied he called to Octavius, who was waiting below, to follow him, and to bring a small satchel of gear José had already prepared, together with a large tin pail and a military-type folding spade. They climbed slowly for most of the morning, zigzagging upward on the loose stony soil and over the decayed but sharp edges of granite outcroppings that extended to right and left at regular intervals across their path. José paused from time to time to fix his bearings on something at the top of the mountain, where weathered granite, heavily fissured and seamed, formed a final vertical wall.

Just below the summit he found what he was looking for. In one of the narrowest fissures, folded into the rock face, a black slit scarcely visible from more than a few feet away, Octavius could now see the bees coming and going, and hear a steady hum from inside the rock. José took the satchel from Octavius and laid out its contents: a stick of dynamite, a couple of blasting caps, three or four feet of black-powder fuse, some matches, a knife, a crimping tool for the blasting caps, a smooth stick about eighteen inches long and, finally, the canteen of water they had brought to drink from. He studied the crevice carefully and the rock around it, probing finally with particular interest a small opening, just a crack, widened at the centre, about two feet down and a little to the left of the bee cave. With the knife he cut the dynamite stick into two unequal pieces. Then he cut off a bit at the end of the length of fuse and stuck the fresh-cut end into a blasting cap and crimped the cap onto the fuse expertly, working with hands to one side and behind him and with his face averted.

He worked the cap with its tail of fuse gently into the cut end of the smaller piece of dynamite, from which he had scooped out some of the explosive filling, and bent the fuse back along the side of the dynamite, so that when he tamped it, open end first, into the little crevice, the fuse and cap held snugly in place. He did this slowly and methodically, with great delicacy of touch, pushing with the stick in one hand and feeding the fuse with the other, until the charge reached a depth that satisfied him. Then he scraped together a small mound of alkali dust from the base of the cliff, made a crater and poured in enough water to make a thick putty-like mud, with which he plastered in the dynamite, filling in the crack around it completely, leaving the black fuse sticking out. An inch back from the free end of the fuse he made a partial cut and bent it on itself, exposing fresh powder that would light readily. He put everything back in the satchel except the matches, one of which he held ready to strike, and motioned to Octavius to pick up the bucket and spade and move along to the shelter of a corner off to the side.

After the thump, which sounded, Octavius said, as though it came from somewhere inside the mountain, not at all the ear-splitting crack he had expected, they went back to have a look. A slab of rock between the dynamited crack and the bee cave had fractured neatly at an angled depth of eight inches to a foot and fallen away, leaving the hive exposed but undamaged, and the bees, thousands of them, lying dead or stunned, all over the surface of the combs and down the slope.

It took two more trips up and down the mountain, that evening and the next morning, to get all the honey within reach, filling the bucket with sticky gobs of honey and beeswax. There was even more they left behind, ancient stuff, black and tarry, some of it hard as rock, smelling of long-dead flowers.

By the time the girl arrived in the pickup with Pra, there was still lots of honey in the bucket, but José had already drifted off, the way he came, walking across the desert. Octavius was sorry to see him go.

5

After José left and just before the arrival of Sylvia, Pra got the assayer's report and a cheque for two thousand dollars from the smelter in El Paso. This was for their first shipment of ore from the Santa Fe siding in Amado, shovelled by hand into an open car, all sixty tons, from the platform where the trucks had dumped it in a series of little hills. When the cheque arrived Pra bought real cigarettes instead of Bull Durham, and enough groceries to satisfy Daniel and Tamayo, as well as paying them their back wages. The Mexicans went home for a weekend with their families. Pra traded in his blue ranch wagon for the white pickup, and the first thing he did with the new truck was take J.B. and Octavius to whoretown in Nogales.

Pra and J.B. and Octavius showered and put on clean clothes at the motel in Amado. In Nogales they went to a barber and got haircuts and shaves, except for Octavius, who only got a haircut, to the merriment of the Mexican barber and his regular customers, who had an idea what his mates had in store for this beardless gringo.

When the three of them got to whoretown it was already dark. The single street was dirt and there were no lights except from dim interiors, weakly illuminating the open doors of the numerous cantinas. They went into the nearest of these and sat down at a table with two whores in flimsy dresses, one young and one old, Indian women, copper-coloured, with short arms and bowed legs, and little breasts perched high on their wide chests. A man with a trumpet and another with an outsized guitar appeared in the doorway and started playing. J.B. squeezed the breasts of the older woman. She didn't like it. He then began stroking her abdomen with his fingers in a peculiar way, and winking at Pra and Octavius, as though to demonstrate a theory about what women liked. The woman edged away and left the table.

Pra lit up a Chesterfield. He looked good in a one-piece jumpsuit, like a mechanic's, but clean and neatly pressed. His blonde hair lay in soft waves. He nodded to the younger woman and they got up and went through a door. J.B., still wearing his hard-hat, got up to look for the other woman. Octavius went outside and wandered up and down the dirt street with a quick, purposive step, to avoid being accosted, although there seemed little danger of that. Figures emerged from the gloom and as quickly disappeared into it again. The slow flat notes of the trumpet, playing something over and over in a minor key, accompanied by the soft sibilant tattoo of the guitar, could be heard from one quarter, then another, insinuating tragedy and transcendence into the night and the cool desert air. Was that laughter? A soft groan? A moist burst of staccato Spanish? One could not be sure of anything, of its direction or meaning.

Pra was still with his girl when Octavius found him in another cantina. J.B. had disappeared.

"Your turn," Pra said. And something else, and something about three dollars.

The girl said something wheedling in Spanish. She had nice eyes with real amusement in them.

Octavius remembers saying "No," in the clipped Spanish way. Then, as the refusal seemed to him to hang harshly in the air, he said more softly, "No. Grácias."

6

After a few days Pra went back to Nogales in the white pickup on some business, and returned with Sylvia. How he found her remained a mystery. No one knew whether he had known of her on some previous visit, or had just picked her up that day. There was speculation in the camp that Pra had bought her in a deal, from someone in a bar.

Sylvia was certainly a town girl, and seemed to have had a respectable upbringing. She was brought in, Pra explained, when they all assembled in the cookhouse that evening, to help out with the food and generally around the cabins. Having got out one carload, and Tamayo insisting they were working a rich deposit of ore with no end in sight, Pra was keen to step up the pace of work and make another carload quickly. This would mean longer shifts for everyone and Octavius could not be spared from the mine, especially with José gone.

The presence of the girl precipitated a number of changes at the mine. Daniel and Tamayo, satisfied for the time with the improvement in the supplies, were happy working the longer hours, and took to preparing their own food at times that suited them. They disdained the company of the gringos and more-or-less refused to acknowledge the presence of the girl, which threw her upon the others, although she spoke almost no English. Octavius knew some Spanish and readily picked up more, and they quickly devised a means of communication. J.B., for obscure reasons of his own, moved his quarters from the building occupied by Daniel and Tamayo to one of the disused dirt-floor shacks, relics of an earlier time, on the far side of the arroyo, where he set himself up in an ostentatious squalor.

J.B. was a long, loose-limbed Cajun, a roughneck Pra had lured away from a Texas oil field. He wore cowboy boots at all times, even in the mine, and his aluminium oil-field hard-hat, to which a miner's lamp could only be fitted awkwardly, and would only sleep naked, which they had discovered already one night in a motel in Patagonia, on the last leg of their first trip together from Texas to Arizona. The three of them, Pra, Octavius and J.B. had had to share a single sagging bed, and kept guns in the bed too, a .22 and a .30-06, because Pra was convinced, perhaps not without reason, that the owner intended to murder them before morning. This was after the carburettor wheezed to a standstill in the middle of the night and they pushed the blue ranch wagon over the continental divide with lungs on fire from the cold and altitude.

Before that they had stopped to visit an old coot with a bushy yellow-stained beard Pra said was Billy the Kid. At least eighty, he lived in an Airstream in the middle of New Mexico with a strapping woman half his age. He was cagey about the Kid part and wouldn't say yes or no, but in exchange for a box of groceries, including everything necessary for a big breakfast for all of them, and which the woman immediately set about to prepare in an assortment of grease-encrusted iron skillets, the Kid told them stories. Among others, how he had discovered, with the aid of a war surplus metal detector, the buried remains of a convoy of German military vehicles—half-tracks, two-and-a-half-tons, artillery pieces—that had been part of an invasion force from Mexico that had been hushed up after the war.

This barminess, Octavius quickly grasped, was not a personal quality but an effect of the West and its spaces and its hallucinations, like the mountains they could see from the Kid's trailer, which, as you stared at them, rose and fell from some trick of atmosphere, soft humps slowly rearing themselves into peaks and then subsiding, at no rate you could detect directly except to note that what was there a few minutes before no longer was, and vice-versa. The landscape inculcated a dreamy credulity, which you saw everywhere you went, and that could turn nasty in a flash. They were chased, Pra and Octavius and J.B., in a West Texas town of flies and irrigation ditches, by six old men with mean faces and varicose legs, out into the dirt street from a former saloon that advertised cancer cures. Pra had brought along his Geiger counter and told the fifteen or twenty old parties sitting around against the uranium-padded walls that there was no more radiation in the walls than there was in sunlight, and offered to demonstrate if they would step outside.

But Pra believed too, and took the shiny cylindrical counter and its heavy battery with him everywhere in case they stumbled on a uranium bonanza, clicking away over right-of-way cuttings, slag heaps, any exposed or eroded rock face, disturbing young prospector families camped over holes in the ground and nothing but tarpaulins for shelter and a suckling brat or two. Pra believed stories of mule trains of Spanish gold, always, it seemed, abandoned in deep shafts between twin peaks, or some other such vague and transparently symbolical place, that needed only to be properly identified and then kept secret while an expedition was formed.

The thread connecting all his schemes was the promise of riches as the reward of persistence and luck. It was not only the Hope Mine on which these dreams rested. Or at least Pra never claimed it was. Nor did he say it wasn't. The Hope Mine was not even a means to an end, it was more like an episode in a drama, and the drama was the life of Antonio Pra, belly gunner in the Pacific, smoker of Chesterfields, a hunter who limited himself fastidiously to bow and arrow and small-bore rifle. He knew about women and he knew about rocks. He never got dirty. Somewhere he kept, as a souvenir of the war, a necklace of Jap teeth. Pra promised nothing, and everything, and expected absolute commitment in return.

Octavius had seen from the first day they picked him up, in an oil field south of San Antonio, that J.B. did not measure up. The way he guzzled beer, the side-of-the-mouth phoney cowboy lingo, the corny jokes and buzz words, his lewd insinuations. Octavius was in part puzzled that Pra did not see this, and in part saw that Pra as leader had to remain above such things. Pra's purity in this regard was his weakness. Octavius kept his thoughts about J.B. to himself, resolving to watch Pra's back.

As soon as they reached the mine the trouble Octavius expected came out in the open. J.B. began complaining about the work, the hours, the Mexicans. They in turn viewed his scheming and malingering—and his sheer, lanky, loud gringoness—with profound contempt. J.B. acquired pains and small injuries. His back hurt, and his feet, mainly due to his insistence on wearing cowboy boots in the mine. He spoke of workers' compensation insurance, paid holidays, legal rights and protections. He saw himself drawing disability payments while installed on a veranda in whoretown in Nogales. Pra coaxed and humoured him, and the truth was he needed him, not only because when J.B. worked he bent himself to it, and could shovel the heavy lead ore for ten, twelve hours at a time, but also because J.B. was a necessary foil, an illustration or lesson for Octavius, which Pra endlessly insinuated. How a guy like J.B. would never amount to anything, never be there at the end, when it all paid off, unlike him, Octavius, who would go all the way, be there at the kill, for the riches, and the women.

7

The trouble with J.B. could not have come at a worse time, as Pra was eager to make the second shipment to El Paso. The arrival of the girl might have freed them from most of the housekeeping chores around the camp, but as it was, and through no fault of her own, she became a new source of friction. J.B. was not content to move across the arroyo to the old camp, he expected the girl to clean up after him, including emptying each morning the tin can he used during the night as a chamber pot, a provocative demand that caused many storms and led very shortly to J.B. quitting the mine altogether and installing himself, as he threatened, and Pra had predicted, in Nogales, from whence he bombarded Pra, through a shyster lawyer in Tucson, with demands for compensation and damages. All of which missives, after the first few, Pra threw away without reading. The final episodes with J.B. at the camp had amused the girl Sylvia more than frightened her, and her knowing grimaces and confidential winks to Octavius further cemented a growing bond between them.

Sylvia was put up in the cabin that Pra and Octavius shared, next to the entrance to the old tunnel that had once been known as the Horseshoe Mine, abandoned when the Hope Mine was first opened. Pra had put a barrier against the tunnel entrance, and padlocked it, and stored cases of dynamite just inside. The cabin had two rooms, one of which was turned over to the girl, who fixed it up as best she could into a private retreat. Octavius and Pra slept in the other room. Pra slipped into the girl's room at night after they were all settled. He was always back in his own bunk by morning. Nothing was said about this by any of them.

Sylvia proved to be extremely neat and clean, and feminine in all her movements and gestures. She was small, and looked even younger than she was. Octavius took her to be the same age as he was, which was fifteen, although Octavius had told Pra he was eighteen. He felt keenly the dual tug that the girl exerted on his inexperienced nature. The powerful sentimental and idealizing impulse which the presence of the girl excited in the boy combined with the urge to seem the older of the two, the mature and protective male. She could not possibly have known the stresses that some of her instinctively teasing gestures placed on him. When they were all together for dinner in the main cabin she would look around to see that the others weren't watching and she would run her hands down over the striped polo shirts Pra had bought her to wear, pressing her small firm breasts as she did so, with a look of sweet satisfaction and a quick glance at Octavius to be sure he had seen.

Octavius knew exactly when and where the girl performed her toilet, which was in the early morning behind their bunkhouse, an affair involving a bench and two galvanized buckets, shampoo and soap and a cloth and a towel. He regarded these precincts as sacred at those times and carried himself as far away as he could. When he wasn't working in the mine he would go far down the arroyo, or out on the desert to the deserted camp, where he kept the Mexican comic book, or sometimes into the Horseshoe Mine, which he got to by a vertical shaft he had discovered up on the hillside, and which was a labyrinth of rotten and fallen timbers and partially collapsed chambers covered in bat droppings. It was connected with the Hope Mine, where they were now working, by means of narrow fissures and seams that Octavius had discovered and kept to himself.

He was aware also of the girl's movements during the day, and conceived an elaborate secret guardianship over her, which consisted chiefly in not inflicting on her his presence, or even the sight of him, except from a distance and as though accidentally or by chance. Above all never looking directly at her and never being seen spying on her, permitting her to feel if anything that she was gazing on him and espying his movements and not the other way around. Always observing strictly his self-imposed taboo, not only about her bathing times, but also when he saw her heading up the arroyo, where they each had a place in the dry stream bed where they relieved themselves. Octavius knew she went a long way farther than any of them, and when he could he made himself visible on her return, at such a distance and in such a quarter that she would know he could not have watched her, and that no one else could have either, without his observing it.

8

Daniel and Tamayo pressed ahead with the blasting in a large stope, a word Octavius learned signified the long, steeply angled, constantly expanding chamber, stepped to permit working on the steep incline, and whose general shape and direction was dictated by the deposit of ore they were removing. This deposit they had first intersected well below the main level and about a quarter of a mile from the entrance of the mine. Ever since, they had been working upwards, following the ore. The ore clung to the underside of a vast porphyry dike, a dark red impenetrable granite mass, gleaming with embedded quartz crystals, that angled up from the depths of the earth and formed one of the regular lines of dark, broken outcroppings visible on the mountainside above.

Twice a day, having drilled overhead into the ore face,

and planted the dynamite charges and lit the fuses, Daniel and Tamayo scrambled down the floor of the stope, crawled through the sliding door in the timber barrier at the bottom, climbed the adjacent vertical shaft by a ladder, alongside the bucket that lifted the ore to the main level, and followed the narrow-gauge track to the entrance on the side of the mountain. Outside, they paused by the big Ingersoll-Rand compressor, and listened, counting on their fingers the dull distant thumps, making sure all the charges had gone off. Back down again, after lunch, or the following morning, they released the fallen ore onto iron sheets, laid there for the purpose, to be shovelled into the bucket and winched up the shaft on a greased timber skid. Once the barrier was clear of fallen ore, Daniel and Tamayo crawled inside and up the stope to the ore face to begin drilling again.

The ore was rich, the lead popping and crackling when the acetylene flame from a miner's headlamp was held to it. The stuff was too heavy for the winch to handle if the bucket was filled more than half way. Shovelling it was back-breaking work. Until he left, it was J.B.'s job to fill the bucket, while Octavius worked the winch that drew it up.

At the top of the shaft, in a niche in the rock reached by a single plank over the open chasm, the operator of the winch, which worked by air piped in from the compressor outside, could, by careful coaxing and tapping of levers, take up or release the cable to raise or lower the bucket on its greased skids. An ingenious but simple device involving lugs on the bucket, and notches and an escape mechanism on the skids, permitted him to tip the contents of the bucket directly into the waiting ore car on its track opposite, and send the empty bucket to the bottom of the shaft.

Octavius got very good at manipulating the winch. His hands moved expertly over the temperamental and dangerous pressure-valve knobs and drum-brake handles, wedged up in his precarious pulpit with his back to the rock wall. Behind the exposed drum and flying cable of the antiquated winch, he made the routine hauling up and down of the prosaic iron bucket a fluent ballet of squealing iron and creaking timber. Not forgetting to call to the man below *Abajo* as the bucket was about to descend, and anticipating his *Arriba* which signified that the bucket was full and could be hauled up.

Three buckets it took to fill the little iron ore car to capacity, then push the car through the tunnel to the outside, man-handling it over the points where spur lines converged. If the load was waste rock Octavius up-ended the car over the edge of the great tailings mound to the left; if ore, he took the right-hand track and tipped the load into the top of the red metal hopper set in the side of the mountain. It was mostly ore now.

Octavius liked to run as fast as he could on his trips out with the ore car. Sometimes in his haste he derailed at the most troublesome of the switch points, and had to brace his back against the top-heavy little car, each end in turn, levering the little flanged wheels and a half-ton of ore onto the track again. Sometimes it took a while for J.B. to fill the bucket; he had to help Daniel and Tamayo with something, or he'd finished shovelling up what was on the iron plates and had crawled up into the timber barrier to release more of the fallen ore. When there was going to be a long wait between one *Arriba* and the next, Octavius used the time to explore unused tunnels and shafts.

The Hope Mine had been worked intermittently for forty or fifty years. Where they were working now was at the farthest point from the entrance ever reached. The other tunnels at this level were all dead ends. The mine had never paid off for its various investors. The present working—it was eighty feet down to the bottom of the bucket shaft—had proven to be the richest find in the history of the mine. The stope in which Daniel and Tamayo were daily blasting out quantities of ore was approaching, and would soon pass, as it angled upward, the main level itself, at which time it would become worthwhile to extend the tunnel further into the mountain to meet it. They could then bring the narrow-gauge track directly underneath the work, with a new timber barrier and chute which would load ore directly into the ore car, avoiding the shovelling and the cumbersome bucket-and-winch business altogether. This was Pra's plan. Octavius listened attentively as Pra worked up the figures to show how much the anticipated ore would amount to, what it would fetch at the smelter, and how they could cannibalise timber and track from unused parts of the mine for the proposed extension.

But Octavius knew something else about what lay ahead in that direction, something he had discovered in his solitary explorations.

9

The first time it was the girl's idea. The thing Octavius had dreamed of but so far had not dared to propose. She was waiting for him one morning by the track where it went out over the hopper, when he came out on his first trip with the ore car, and motioned to him that she wanted to go down into the mine with him.

Their communications now consisted of an efficient scheme of looks and gestures and a growing stock of Spanish words and phrases and some English. Sylvia taught him phrases in Spanish, in the evenings, with many suppressed giggles, because of the others. She had grown easy with him. Whatever shyness she possessed was born of a tactical reserve rather than timidity. She was trying out a power at which she was only inexperienced, but not untalented or unwilling. For his part, Octavius could not tell if his elaborate exercises in tactfulness had earned him this intimacy or not. Perhaps up to a point they had. The deeper truth was certainly that Octavius was in love with his own feelings, and these feelings were chaste and idealizing. His true talent was for worship. His methods were not ruses but ends in themselves. They were both children, Octavius and Sylvia, but in very different ways, and of the two of them she had the more supple and playful intelligence. Sylvia wrote on scraps of paper in the evening under the kerosene lamp, while Daniel and Tamayo twittered together in their faintly sinister way. She wrote *te quiero*, sometimes *yo te quiero*, or *yo te quiero a ti*, and handed these slips to Octavius, pleased with herself, trying out these declarations of love as though they were exercises in penmanship, teasing Octavius the while for his perpetually sober, tender face and dirty neck. Octavius didn't mind. He was captivated.

And so Octavius readily agreed, that morning in early spring, to take Sylvia with him into the mine. This was the week before J.B. left for Nogales. Pra was away for the day. From the laboured, nearly constant roar of the big Ingersoll-Rand, Octavius could tell that Daniel and Tamayo had begun drilling.

They stopped just inside the mine entrance, where a little chamber off to one side held a few days' supply of blasting equipment: the dynamite, caps and fuse and the crimping tools, and the tin drums of carbide for the miners' lamps. Octavius showed her these things without a word, pointing and gesturing to indicate the functions of the simple and deadly devices. The girl stared and nodded. Octavius took an empty dynamite box and set it in the empty ore car, then helped her gently into the car and sat her on the box, facing forward, only her head showing above the sides, her white knuckles gripping the forward edge.

The little car clicked over the rails without a hitch, to the steady shush of steel on steel. The points for once presented no difficulties, as Octavius anticipated each hazard, smoothly canting the top-heavy trolley this way and that by shifting his weight, exaggerating it a little, as much in joy as for showing off. He turned up the drip on his carbide lamp so that the tongue of flame shot out its maximum length with a loud hiss, illuminating the tunnel far ahead with a dancing light, reflecting back a gleam from the girl's oiled black hair, and picking out her delicate fingers resting on the edge of the car.

Octavius said he had wanted this journey to last forever. He felt at one with the unwieldy car, guiding it with the lightest of touches, his feet adjusting to the uneven and narrow sleepers with unconscious ease. They sped past old crazy shafts disappearing darkly upwards. Over the places where the floor was thin, where, he knew, just inches below his hurrying feet slumbered dark abysses, deep places of old rock-falls and splintered timbers into which he might at any moment be hurled when the tunnel floor gave way, as it must surely one day.

His trips alone with the car, he said, were always a race with his fear of death. He imagined terrible things: explosions, projectiles, jagged cutting things, hurtling, impaling things from the dark. He struck bargains with God: another five seconds of safety, ten seconds, fifteen; holding back catastrophe by the smallness and insignificance of his requests, as though God would not be bothered to crush him for a matter of mere seconds—his reckoning, he said, with the vengeful theology of the chapel-world of his childhood. He hedged these bets with a fighter's coiled awareness, a dancer's poise, ready, every moment, although his worn-out and oversize boots were loose and heavy on his feet, to spring aside at the last moment from these mortal dangers as though on wings.

And now all this practice, these dreams, this acute mental work and suffering, had materialized this moment, his pushing this girl deep into the mountain in her own iron chariot. He would have held up the mountain, had it threatened to fall on her, with an outstretched arm, or with a mighty shout. The intimations that had stirred in his unformed soul had now found their object, in those white knuckles and gleaming black head.

All this Octavius told me in a state of peculiar exaltation. This memory, of all his memories, had never for one moment left him. He had been there beneath the mountain with the girl at any time he chose these last fifty years.

When they arrived at the bucket shaft, Octavius could hear J.B. down below, scraping ore out of the timber barrier and singing one of his tuneless ballads. Daniel and Tamayo were high up inside the stope. The rapid reciprocating cough of the pneumatic drill, every day approaching nearer the main level, had advanced so far that the muffled sound, more a vibration than a noise, seemed now from below, now from somewhere ahead. Octavius's senses were attuned as never before to what he knew the girl was seeing and feeling for the first time: the grotesque shapes of the winch and the skids, and the dark hole and the surrounding rocks—skittering across their vision in the uncertain light of Octavius's lamp—the coppery taste of ore on the tongue when you breathed through your mouth, the pervasive acetylene stench of carbide, the soft hiss of escaping air around the winch. Octavius helped the girl out of the car and felt the goose-flesh on her thin arms. She hugged herself, making her small breasts push up under the striped knitted shirt, a kind of boy's shirt Pra had bought for her. She was not afraid. Her eyes were shining with excitement and her nostrils flared. Octavius led her across the plank, and they squeezed together onto the little bench behind the winch. Octavius sat very still, conscious of the girl's hip and thigh against his, and concentrated on J.B.'s next *Arriba*.

10

Pra came back from Tucson with a mining equipment salesman and when they went away again, Pra took Sylvia with him in the white pickup. He said she needed more clothes. When they returned, Sylvia had parcels in her arms. She disappeared at once into the cabin she shared with Pra and Octavius, and Octavius didn't see her for the rest of that day.

The next morning, Pra left again for Tucson and the girl was waiting for Octavius on his first trip out with the ore car. He said nothing. He glanced at her only sideways and fleetingly. He did not wait to see whether she wanted to go down into the mine again. Something told him not to force or to rush whatever it was that was moving towards him or towards which he was moving. His feeling had deepened since their trip into the mountain, although he could not have said precisely what that feeling was, other than that it disturbed him. He had not been to the camp out in the desert for several weeks, although he could remember in detail the pneumatic and always tearful heroines of the Mexican comic book. He thought of them now, and thought of Sylvia in her new clothes, and then of the whores in Nogales, especially the young ones, and recalled the loose talk between J.B. and Pra, about how these girls were likely all *novias* of boys in their distant villages, and how Mexicans had no feeling about this, because they were poor and they were Catholics with many children, many girls to provide for. The girls would go home and set up as wives from their earnings as whores, and everybody knew, but would never say anything, so no harm was done. Octavius thought this infinitely tragic, these tainted brides and tainted nest-eggs. The worst was imagining these girls in the arms of someone like J.B. Pra was different. He was clean and attractive, and respectful to people, including whores. Although Octavius could not approve of everything Pra did, he accepted that there was somewhere in these matters a law of life that took precedence over a too fastidious view, and of which he, Octavius, had only an imperfect understanding and was only on the threshold of grappling with.

It was like that too with killing, a thing Pra had explained to Octavius over and over again. Honour, sportsmanship—even aesthetic considerations—required that the hunter use only the minimum force, with the maximum risk to himself. The bow-and-arrow and the small calibre rifle were Pra's weapons. He mostly used a .22 carbine for the hunt—he claimed he would have been satisfied with the single-shot version he used as a boy—an austere self-restraint that meant getting as close as possible to the animal, risking only head shots and shots to the heart, and only at close range, and being prepared to track a wounded animal as long as was necessary, even for many hours or days, to be sure of the kill and prevent unnecessary suffering or waste. The essential thing was respect for the life of the animal. Having decided to take that life in a certain fashion, you were responsible for all the consequences. Octavius acknowledged in his heart the superiority of this severe and beautiful ethic and supposed it originated in B-29s over the Pacific and that generation of beautiful men smoking cigarettes and killing Japs with their tail-guns and belly-guns.

Octavius could not kill anything. He had felt Pra's disappointment when they eased up within easy distance of a white-tail or mule deer by the side of the track, and Octavius had the .22 and he waited too long and the tail went up and the deer bounded away. On these occasions Pra had been as much puzzled as angry.

Pra spoke also of virgins. Not boastfully, but as one will tell exemplary and instructive tales. Of a virgin in the cotton fields around Harlingen, in Texas, where Pra grew up. A cherry, he said, a white leg over the back of the front seat of her '32 coupe at the end of the row, and how every day she showed up at the end of the rows he was cultivating that day, and there in the coupe he did it for her every day, which was how virgins were, and what they needed. You became responsible for them. Octavius listened as to something interesting and no doubt true, but beyond him, like the perfect head shot or the clean heart shot. As much as he conceded to the dead buck and to the virgin of the cotton rows an ethical seriousness rooted in the facts of the world, the power of the kill was not given to him. Octavius had heard men and boys talking dirty, but when Pra said the little whore in whoretown was tight like a coke bottle, or described to him the white leg of the virgin, thrown over the seat of the '32 coupe, these were facts, states of affairs that actually existed in the world and that made certain demands.

11

It was several days after Pra bought Sylvia the new clothes that J.B. had left for Nogales in a final burst of imprecations and threats, at which Pra shrugged contemptuously. Octavius was, on balance, happy to see the back of the roughneck and his idiot cowboy saws and tuneless singing, and his night cans of piss set out for Sylvia in the morning by his filthy cabin across the arroyo. Pra took J.B. away early in the morning in the white pickup and returned with a coloured man who had an Indian wife and three small children in a shack in Amado. The man had been hired before to help shovel ore at the railway siding, but he had never been in a mine and was frightened of going underground. Pra was amused at the idea of putting a black man in a mine and made sly jests about white eyeballs and teeth shining in the dark. Nevertheless, the new man took his position mucking at the bottom of the bucket shaft and learned to say *Arriba* and *Abajo* to the amazement of Daniel and Tamayo.

Getting the new man installed was going to take up the afternoon, and the water and gasoline drums had to be filled, a time consuming affair that needed to be done every two or three days—even more frequently with the amount of drilling going on—so Pra sent Octavius back to Amado with the pickup. When Octavius passed their cabin on the way out, Sylvia was waiting in the shadow of the abandoned mine entrance. She motioned for him to stop, and ran out and climbed in beside him. This was their first time alone together since the trip into the mine.

Octavius had learned to drive on the trip from Texas in the blue ranch wagon with its twitchy Ford clutch. Somewhere around Aguas Prietas, in the early hours after midnight, Pra had climbed over into the back, where J.B. was already asleep, and Octavius applied what he had seen Pra do. With a minimum of grinding and lurching he had got the ranch wagon under way. By morning he was pretty good at it.

He could now handle the white pickup with unstudied efficiency. He said little to Sylvia the twenty miles to the filling station at Amado, opening and shutting the five cattle gates by himself. On the return trip with the loaded drums, when Octavius got out to open the last gate, which was situated on a rise, at the beginning of the long ascent into the hills, Sylvia signalled that she needed to stop. A low ridge to one side of the road afforded some shade. Octavius sat on a projecting bit of rock and waited while Sylvia went around to the other side of the ridge. When she returned she sat down a little distance from Octavius, clearly in no hurry to move on.

"I hate them," she said, in a violent burst of English, grimacing at her feet, which she held straight out in front of her and turned this way and that.

"Boys' shoes," she said, in Spanish this time. He followed her gaze. They certainly were boys' shoes. Reddish-brown leather with a raised U-shaped welt of white threads around each toe, and thick brown woven laces. Octavius considered this. Her small feet accentuated the boyishness of these shoes, which were practical enough, but neither were they work boots or outdoor boots. They were ordinary daytime shoes, school shoes, ugly shoes. Pra had bought these for her. Octavius looked down at his own shoes, stained engineer boots, stiff and cracked from repeated soaking and drying. He had no socks in them, as the only socks he had had rotted away long ago.

He kept his eyes on these boots of his as Sylvia talked, a sing-song in Spanish and English without inflection or let-up, like a mud dam collapsing and letting all sorts of rubbish loose in a sluggish torrent. She pointed as she talked, variously, down the road to Amado, with an airy wave of her hand to the south indicating where she had come from, perhaps Nogales, then to points in the clearing around them, including the white pickup, the gate, a place against the low ridge, and then up the road toward the mine. When she ran down she started all over again.

At some point, out of this repetitious jumble, Octavius understood the girl was saying Pra had raped her, pulled her out of the truck and forced himself on her, here in this clearing, the day Pra brought her to the mine, the day Octavius had seen her in the white pickup from his vantage point across the arroyo by the old cabins.

Octavius had at first no coherent thought about what he was hearing. His mouth turned dry and he felt his chest constrict. His stomach was sucked into a hard small knot and he thought for a while he was going to vomit.

A threshold had been crossed. Everything he had thought until now would have to be re-evaluated in the light of this image and this idea. But he desperately needed from somewhere the instinct and strength and wisdom of a man, and needed it right now. He had to act the man, somehow, in front of this girl. The moment he had long fantasised had arrived, in a form and at a time he was not prepared for. There was no one here to fight, and nowhere to run to, and he had no time. He needed to do something at once to assert his control of the situation, no matter how inadequate or illogical. He had an inspiration. He would show Sylvia his secret.

12

Octavius dropped Sylvia off at the cabin and drove on to the mine entrance. He backed the pickup to a point above the Ingersoll-Rand, screwed the cap off the gasoline drum, inserted a rubber hose and sucked on the other end to start the siphoning. When the gas gurgled nearly to his lips he quickly stuck the free end into the compressor gas tank. Then he emptied the two water drums into the reservoir that supplied water to the drills. When these chores were done he went to fetch his hard-hat and his lamp from the supply room just inside the mine entrance. He filled the bottom of the lamp with carbide from the tin drum and filled the top with water. He could tell from the frequent labouring of the compressor engine that Daniel and Tamayo were still drilling. They would be finishing soon and then setting the last charge of the day.

When he got back to the cabin Sylvia was waiting for him. Octavius picked up the padlock key and opened the barrier to the old Horseshoe Mine.

Octavius led the way, taking Sylvia by the hand over the fallen rubble, to a place where a dim crepuscular light filtered down a crooked shaft partly clogged with rotting timbers, and powdered bat guano settled on them and burned in their nostrils. Octavius oriented himself and then set off through the maze of tunnels, bearing mainly to their right, Octavius never hesitating when a choice was to be made, sometimes crawling over debris reaching nearly to the roof of the tunnel. Once, Octavius's lamp went out. He unhooked it from his hat and felt for the lever that regulated the drip of water. He shook the lamp gently. When he heard the steady hiss of gas he moved his thumb over the lighter-wheel on the rim of the reflector. The tongue of yellow-white flame leaped up between them.

Their destination was a remote exploratory tunnel, abandoned perhaps at the time the mine itself had been closed. The end wall was unfinished and jagged. A few remaining drill-holes suggested that the work had been left off abruptly and never resumed. There was no evidence of ore at the work face. Nothing apparently of interest.

To the left side, however, almost at the end of the tunnel, behind a roughly fractured protrusion of porphyry, on which flakes of iron pyrites glinted in the acetylene lamplight, Octavius pointed at a narrow fissure, easy to overlook and easy to mis-gauge as to depth. It seemed, as he shone the light into it, to be only two or three feet deep and as much in height. But when he squeezed himself into the fissure, and slowly straightened up, all of him but his legs disappeared from Sylvia's view into what was clearly a much larger space above him and tucked under the massive porphyry dike. The light from Octavius's lamp made dancing shadows around his legs, then disappeared, then shone down again, and when it did his legs had disappeared and his voice, in a hollow boom, was telling her to join him.

They lay side by side on finely crushed crystals, as on a bed of opal sand or of ground barley-sugar. They looked up at the roof and sides of an oblong chamber. The air was cool and fresh. The flame in Octavius's lamp guttered in a draught upward to some hidden chimney where the roof slanted into the porphyry dike, connecting perhaps directly with the mountainside above, or with one of the old vertical shafts. What they saw as they lay there quietly, took away speech and even thought.

Over every surface of the chamber, over every square inch of the walls and ceiling, dancing and shape-shifting in the eerie light of Octavius's lamp, glowed and sparkled a translucent mineral in thin, sharp, rectangular plates, heaped and jumbled together, intersecting and superimposed in a weird architecture of random angles, held together as though by magnetic attraction, or as though a million million stone butterflies had lighted in this small room. The dominant colour was a warm greyish-yellow amber, a colour of ash and clay mixed, of fossilized bone or of very old ivory. Here and there a brownish-red predominated, or a smoky red-purple. The plates were extremely fragile to the touch. Reaching up anywhere produced a small shower of glittering dust and flakes. The bed on which they lay was accounted for by Octavius's previous visits, when he discovered he could not enter the chamber except by crushing the undisturbed plates on the floor, and so had made a thorough job of it.

At last the cool air made the girl shudder and squeeze her arms together up against her breasts. Octavius removed his hat and put his ear to the floor of the cave. Daniel and Tamayo were getting close.

13

On the second day after Octavius had shown Sylvia the wulfenite cave, a fine layer of snow fell overnight on the desert that evaporated quickly and left a sharp smell in the nose and a trick of vision in which near and far things were the same, and the eye lost its capacity to judge distance or height. Octavius could see the white pickup coming from miles out, long before the noise of it reached him, the plume of dust disappearing when it dipped into the dry arroyos, the windows glinting where the sun caught it coming over the rises. It would be another half-hour before Pra arrived, allowing for the two gates between the boy and the approaching truck, gates that had to be opened and then shut again.

Allowing also for the extra weight of the drums of water and gas, and the cases of dynamite and the other stuff, the carbide and fuses and blasting caps, he'd picked up in Tucson that morning. Pra drove carefully when he was loaded like that.

There had not been until today an opportunity to get Pra alone and to confront him, as Octavius knew he had to do and had resolved to do. He was not clear in his mind how he would manage it or even whether he could manage it, but his will was firm. This was the moment. He would know what to do.

Octavius brought the .22 up and jammed his cheek against the middle of his thumb, bent taut around the slender part of the stock just below the rear sight. Pra had taught him to do it this way, so the rifle was fused with your skull and where you looked your head went and where your head went the barrel went. He had learned to aim with both eyes open, and to line up the target with the sights in a single movement, beginning already to pull on the stiff trigger, so that the mild kick of the .22 on his cheekbone arrived at exactly the same moment as the aligned images coalesced. He remembered shooting, he said, into the late afternoon sun, the path of the bullet a visible streak, a flat greasy parabola from the crack of the little repeater to the whine far below where the bullet glanced off a discarded oil drum already pocked with innumerable shallow grey dents.

The magazine held ten more rounds, but Octavius had had

enough. One hand holding the rifle and the other stretched out behind to balance with, he slid and scrambled down the slope, breaking off pieces of the thin bitter soil as he went, sending a small shower of stones and dust ahead. He stopped at a shelf just above the entrance to the old mine. To his right a projecting flank of the mountain shielded him from sight from anyone approaching along the road. Directly to his front the road was partly obscured by the tin roof of the bunkhouse he shared with Pra and Sylvia. Pra would drive another quarter mile up and to the left, where the giant rock pile spilled into the valley, and the cluster of sheds and machinery marked the entrance to the Hope Mine. Pra might just catch a glimpse of him as he drove past, but Octavius made no effort to conceal himself. He squatted on the timber lintel, as dry and grey as the dirt above it, placed the rifle carefully across his knees and rested his forearms on it. Octavius said the idea of shooting Pra as he went by had entered his mind. He had even raised the little rifle experimentally, and trained it on the spot where Pra would appear momentarily in his sights, knowing even as he did so that he could not shoot.

When Pra had gone by in the white pickup without seeing him, the boy put the .22 away in the bunkhouse and walked up to the main camp.

14

Pra studied Octavius. "You want to leave?"

Octavius hadn't said anything. He knew that anything he tried to say would undo him. He wouldn't say what he meant to say. He wouldn't finish what he had to say. What he had to do was beginning to form in his mind, but it was best to let it work out as it would. Maybe he was letting Pra have a chance to do something, or to undo something, to set things off on a different path from the one that lay ahead.

Pra teased, but his eyes were hard. "You want to go join J.B.? Sit up there on a veranda in whoretown looking to get something for nothing?

"If you're upset about something, say what it is. I thought we understood each other. You know this mine isn't the end of it. Not like for Daniel and Tamayo. This is all they're ever gonna do. They're happy with that. You can make something out of yourself."

Octavius still said nothing. He felt a queer lassitude creep over him. He was tempted to surrender. He saw everything Pra was doing, and loved him in this moment as never before.

"Is it the girl that's bothering you?"

Pra lit a Chesterfield and pulled a speck of tobacco off his lower lip. He felt he was on good ground and probed further. Everything he said came out with a little pause after it, a hesitation, as though thinking through on the fly some puzzling and difficult problem.

"Nookie is a good thing. When it comes along. Just so you know it isn't everything."

Pra picked his way carefully.

"You been talking to her," Pra said, as a man would who sees everything now, and what he sees has made him reflective, and a little weary.

"She likes you, you know. Hell, all you got to do to get some of that is clean yourself up a bit.

"Wouldn't do you any harm with Daniel and Tamayo, either."

Pra walked to the window by the cook stove and looked up toward the mine entrance. He kept his back to Octavius as he talked.

"They don't like working with you, Daniel and Tamayo. It isn't just the food they complain about. They wanted me to get rid of you. They don't want you working around them. They think you're unlucky. I defended you. You didn't know that, did you?"

Pra turned toward Octavius now, fishing some crumpled bills from his pocket.

"You want your money now? I'll give you what's coming

to you, even though you didn't earn all of it. Here's a hundred dollars and I got another hundred in the cabin. You take it, we're all square and no hard feelings. Something big happens then it's just too bad. You just made your choice and that's that."

Pra was in little doubt of the outcome as he studied Octavius's flushed and staring face, waiting for the moment when Octavius would quit staring and look down. When he did, Pra's voice dropped lower, became softer. He chuckled lightly, just a catch in the voice, as when something humorous is shared between men who understand one another without effort.

"I don't know what to do with you sometimes. You don't make it easy.

"I had to watch out for a guy like you in the war. I kept him alive just so he could lose his cherry proper.

"Now listen, kid, let's first get this load out to the smelter."

Pra became animated.

"The Mexicans sniff paydirt up that stope. They figure this blast today will fill the hopper. The ore is high grade and loose up in there. Mostly cerrusite, they say, with lots of silver in it. We'll all do the mucking for a few days, get that hopper topped up, and when the load is shipped we'll take a break. Go down to Baja for a week and do some deep-sea fishing.

"And don't let that girl get you in a knot. You take her for a while. I'll stay out of the way.

"I know she tells you things. She gets mad at me sometimes. Maybe she put up a little fight at the beginning. But that's all part of the game. She's a hot little thing. A little fish in the bed. Wiggles the whole time.

"Remember, just keep your mind on what's important."

It was impossible for Octavius to counter what Pra was saying with an argument, or with a counter-attitude, or with a direct challenge. Octavius had not staked a claim to Sylvia of the kind that other men are constrained to honour. He had no standing as her protector. He was comical in his transparency. He lacked the dignity of age or position. What would he defend Sylvia with? Could he trust her, and what was there between them on which he could count? The whole edifice of his inner life was an insubstantial dream, a mere feather against the iron realism of Pra. What grew within him now was simply a pressure, a rapidly expanding pressure everywhere inside him, rising from his stomach to his chest to his throat.

Pra went on talking. Octavius gradually tuned him out and became focused instead on the sound of the Ingersoll-Rand on the hillside. It would need new points soon. The valve clearances needed adjusting. There was a cough every time the engine revved up to restore pressure. Listening for this cough made him notice when the engine quit kicking in.

It had been idling for a while now. That meant Daniel and Tamayo were done drilling. They would be dismantling the jacks that held the big overhead drill in position and disconnecting the air and water hoses. It would take time for them to arrange the dynamite charge. A big charge, Pra had said, the last until this load of ore went out. Thirty or forty holes it would be, eight or ten feet deep, arranged in a pattern and set to go off just so, different holes with different charges, some with three or four sticks, some seven or eight. Tamayo made these decisions. Daniel did the cutting of the fuse and crimping on of the blasting caps, the delicate insertion of the caps into the sticks, the tamping, the plugging with mud, the arrangement of the fuse ends so they could be conveniently lit in the right sequence. In the midst of the spluttering and smoke of burning fuse, they would scramble down through the barrier door, then climb up the bucket-shaft ladder, and walk the quarter-mile out. No more than an hour.

Octavius made his decision. The inevitable one, really, he saw with sudden clarity.

15

Octavius's account of what happened at the Hope Mine that winter and spring may be swiftly concluded.

When Pra finishes his speech in the cookhouse, Octavius tells Pra he has something to show him, letting Pra think the issue of the girl, and of Octavius's leaving, is settled. He leads Pra through the labyrinth of the old abandoned mine to the wulfenite cave. He employs a route less direct than the one he used with Sylvia, believing Pra does not know these passages as well as he does. Pra will be disoriented in such a way that he will not realize that the cave hangs on the same porphyry dike as the vein of ore Daniel and Tamayo are working. Octavius has worked out to his satisfaction that the wulfenite cave lies directly in the path of their blasting. Whoever is in the cave at the time the blast goes off will be dragged down the stope and crushed under tons of lead ore. The possibility of success of this scheme is enhanced by the fortuitous period of silence between the end of the drilling and the blast itself, within which anyone standing in the cave will not be warned of the danger.

Octavius considers blocking the exit from the cave to ensure Pra cannot escape once Octavius has got him inside, but there is nothing on the spot to do it with. Instead Octavius finds a pretext for leaving Pra alone in the cave and runs to safety. He waits just inside the barrier at the entrance of the old Horseshoe Mine until he hears the series of dull thuds deep underground that means the charges have gone off. He walks the twenty miles to Amado, leaving behind the girl and the Mexican miners to discover the accident. From Amado he catches a ride to Tucson, and with the money Pra had thrust upon him buys new clothes and takes a train back East.

In a general way this ending is corroborated by something Octavius told me many years ago, as prelude to a quite different story. About a train from Tucson, and that that was how he came to be alone in Grand Central Station one Easter Sunday morning.

Octavius may not have been correct, of course, in his assumptions about the location of the cave in relation to the stope the Mexican miners were working, or the probable effects of the blast. This part of his story may simply not be plausible. Then Octavius seems not to have noticed that killing Pra, as he believed he had done, and then running away, was betraying and abandoning Sylvia, leaving her to face this horror alone, without even a farewell. There was no apparent regret in him about this. No curiosity, even to the end of his life—so far as I know—about what became of Sylvia.

It makes little difference now whether or not Pra was killed in a dynamite explosion in a mine in Arizona in 1956. Or who—or what—caused the disturbance over the wulfenite collection at the university museum in Tucson. Pra had reappeared, like a spectre in an old revenge tragedy. It was not guilt, or remorse, but fear that brought Octavius to my door.

16

Some final pieces of the puzzle of Octavius's life came into my hands after I had already finished this chronicle.

Octavius had no family. The executor of his modest estate was a partner in the investment banking house for which he worked off and on on a contract basis. One day I had a message on my answer machine from his secretary to call him on a matter concerning Mr. Steven's effects.

The address, when we had fixed an appointment, turned out to be one of those discreet limestone and wrought-iron façades with a brass plate in the East Seventies, a branch of something with offices in Zurich and Milan. Our interview was pleasant. The man across from me, breathing integrity and discretion, began by saying that the estate consisted almost entirely of cash and readily negotiable securities. Octavius owned no property. There were books and art works; mostly, as I knew, things that meant something personal to Octavius, and otherwise reflected a refined taste, but nothing very valuable. These things had been sent to auction. Octavius had left a small bequest to his housekeeper, and something larger to a female cousin, the daughter of his mother's sister, who had been his sole relation. The rest went to a variety of cultural institutions, mostly musical.

Since I was not named in Octavius's will, he went on to say, after a delicate pause, there was not, in the ordinary course, any reason to divulge its contents to me. Furthermore, he was not sure quite what the legal position was in regard to what he was about to propose. In glancing through Octavius's private papers, however, he saw that I was Octavius's chief correspondent. It seemed to him that I was the logical person to have these papers. He had discussed it with the cousin named in Octavius's will and she had agreed. This was to be purely a private matter; the papers were not listed in the assets of the estate and nor would the firm's lawyers, who were handling the settlements, know anything of it. Was I willing to take custody of these papers on these terms. Naturally I agreed.

I received a single cardboard file box, somewhat battered and dusty. As soon as I got it home I gave its contents a cursory examination. Packed in tightly and filling the box were bundles of papers tied together with string, the thicker ones flat, some of the more slender bundles rolled up, but each with a cover sheet on which was written some identifying remark together with dates. I removed a few from the top, enough to see that the older bundles were at the bottom and looked as though they had not been disturbed for a long time. My name appeared on several of the bundles, and I recognized my customary blue stationery.

It was several days before I found time to turn to the box again, with no more intention than to take everything out and see if there might be a better order to put things in, and perhaps transfer the contents to a new filing case. I pulled out the bundles with my name on them and set them aside. I spread the rest of them out on the floor, arranging as I went according to the dates written on the cover sheets. Some bundles seemed to consist of nothing but mementos and ephemera—ticket stubs, menus, timetables—from trips he had taken. Others had names, mostly of women.

I decided to save my own letters to him—to keep with the ones I had received from him over the years—and to burn all the rest. I had begun throwing these others back in the box, when I saw something in the bottom I had overlooked. An oilskin wallet, discoloured and cracked, of the kind once issued by travel agents for keeping passports and travel documents together, it had the name and address of such an agent printed in gold letters on the cover, an address in Sunset Park in Brooklyn.

Inside the wallet were a number of papers and photographs, which I spread out carefully, preserving as best I could their original order. A seaman's papers—documents issued by various port constabularies around the world dating from the early 1920s, a letter of reference from a first mate saying that the holder, an able-bodied seaman, was "sober and industrious," a certificate of completion of some obligatory Norwegian naval training—all issued to one Ragnar Sivertsen, Octavius's father, to whom the wallet must have belonged. The other documents were of little interest. I turned to the photographs.

One of these is a wedding picture, a studio photograph. The bride is sitting on a bench. She is wearing a simple dress and a small hat. She holds a round bouquet at her waist. You can see that one of her legs is wasted, and shorter than the other, and requires a heavy orthopedic shoe. The groom, standing behind her, is slight of build, lantern-jawed and big-eared with round pale eyes that droop a bit at the outer corners and fine, light hair flopped across a high brow. His only good feature is a rather fine and slender nose. He is by no means in his first youth, but there is an air of something unformed about him. The suit he is wearing looks brand new and stiff and his hands, which are working man's hands, protrude stiffly from his shirt cuffs.

The groom is the same person as the boy in the official photographs in the seaman's documents. He is also one of the young men in snaps of an outing taken at a Coney Island swimming pool and bath house, all in identical old-fashioned two-piece bathing costumes rented from the establishment, defenceless young men in the absurd woollen bathing suits, the rickety legs and sallow complexions of their luckless generation. The boy I pick out as Ragnar Sivertsen, Octavius's father, is diffident, inexperienced, ill-at-ease even among these ill-at-ease young men, looking into the camera with the same bewildered stare as in his wedding picture.

There are two other pictures in the wallet. One a clipping from a newspaper or handbill, carefully folded, now yellow and brittle. The image is grainy, but you can see the subject must have been a striking, perhaps beautiful, young woman. She is standing next to a wooden lectern, one forearm resting on it, the hand gracefully dangling at the front, the other hand at her side. She is hatless, and dressed with a minimum of ornamentation. The effect is theatrical, understated, at once modest and seductive. A lady preacher or evangelist. Something to do no doubt with the religious society in Sunset Park that Octavius had run away from.

The other photograph is difficult to convey a proper sense of, and even more difficult to account for. The photo is encased in a small metal frame. Octavius's mother, the Italian married to the awkward Norwegian bachelor and shortly to die in childbirth, younger here than in her wedding photo, only a girl, really, she has been posed in a studio as though for some great tragic role—Norma, say, or Bérénice—barefoot, draped in a classical gown or shift, and with a wreath of leaves in her hair. A foot, her crippled one, is resting on a low stool. One hand is touching something, or reaching for something, beyond the edge of the photo, which has been cropped. Absurd and touching. A cruel joke or burlesque perhaps, transformed by the passage of time and the dignity that belongs to the dead into an enigma, the lost key to everything.

I return again and again, as I have at leisure pondered this story and its many loose ends, to the girl Sylvia, and in particular, strange as it may seem, to the episode of the shoes, the ugly shoes that Pra bought for her. This is the detail that provoked her to tell Octavius about Pra's assault on her. There was an insult in those shoes that touched her deeply. Antonio Pra, smoker of Chesterfields, belly-gunner over the Pacific, student of all things to do with women, underestimated, perhaps fatally, the fifteen-year-old Sylvia, the girl in a white pickup in the centre of an alkali waste in the burning sun.

Brother Bringsrud

Rich and beautiful people sit in a modern concert hall in a European capital. Row upon row of white ties and medals, diamond tiaras, flat bosoms in satin dresses. The people are intent on a man playing a piano. The pianist is old and apparently frail; his eyes are shut as though in pain or weariness, or in an excess of inwardness. Nevertheless, he is hitting the keys of the piano with a force that lifts him bodily from the bench.

There are other films in the stack of tin boxes kept in a cupboard to one side of the low platform: travelogues from Norway, temperance films, home movies of missionaries in China or Africa in which white women in round eyeglasses and stout shoes and sly native co-workers, yellow or black as the case may be, stand together or walk about in dumbshow conversation for long minutes.

One or two of these entertainments are shown toward the close of the meetings at the Blue Cross Mission on the first Thursdays of every month. Brother Bringsrud finishes his sermon, then the caretaker of the mission, Old Tom, who lives upstairs and keeps a parrot chained to a roost, sets up a small projector in the aisle between the few rows of assorted wooden and metal folding chairs and pulls down a window blind that serves as a screen.

While Old Tom is about these preparations Sister Ruth and Sister Hildegard retire to a place at the rear of the platform, from which presently come the smells of coffee percolating and of buttered rye-bread and brown goat-milk cheese. At the end of the film cups and saucers and little spoons are distributed. The sisters pour coffee, and cream and lump sugar and plates of open sandwichesare passed around, of goat cheese, or sliced egg and anchovy, or dark salted beef. After an interval and a refilling of the coffee cups, plates of almond pastry appear, carefully sliced, thick or thin, according to how the sisters estimate it has to stretch.

There is never a very large crowd. The bums, all regulars, will sleep in the hall later, on the cots that Old Tom brings to replace the folding chairs. Mostly there are the people from Ebenezer. Besides Brother Bringsrud, Sister Ruth and Sister Hildegard, there are Sister Doris, who plays guitar and sings, and Sister Sara, who only sings. Happy Hansen is always there, called this because her testimony always begins "I am so happy," after which it is unintelligible and soon ends in confusion and sobbing. Then there is a woman who has hair on her face and looks like a cat, and a small man with a twisted mouth, Kjell, who plays the trumpet and seldom speaks and is thought to be mentally disturbed, and Danish Andersen, a short round man who plays the banjo-mandolin, my father and my brother and me.

The history of Ebenezer, which many of these people attend on Sundays, is obscure, because the Free Friends do not keep membership lists. Such history as it had before about 1935 must be gleaned from back copies of *Nordisk Tidende*, in which black edged boxes from time to time announce "special" meetings in one rented hall or another above the shops on Fifth Avenue. In 1935 the Friends purchased a building and Brother Thornquist invited an American from Pennsylvania to be pastor, with his wife, who played the piano. They introduced services in English, and American songbooks, evangelists, gospel rallies and Sunday school, none of which is strictly according to scripture. Ebenezer now has a woman preacher from Canada who has not only doubled the scope of these activities but added a radio ministry. The Friends do not approve of the direction things have taken. Even Brother Thornquist moved to Staten Island when he saw what he had done. On the other hand the Friends believe you can have only one local church during your life. Even if you move away you are still a member of the place where you were saved, even though that place has no membership list. In time they will get rid of the woman preacher, through some talk started by a malicious sister. Ebenezer will be restored to the Friends except that members with children will go to Elim, as my parents did in 1948. Elim is connected with the Filadelfia people, the Pentecostal Friends, whose rivalry with the Free Friends goes back to the early part of the century in Norway.

In 1941 Elim left the old movie house it occupied on Seventh Avenue, just a block from the Blue Cross Mission, and moved into a Jewish Temple on Fourth Avenue. It is now just around the corner from Ebenezer. Elim keeps membership lists and has adopted, after much debate and determined opposition, a songbook with the notes printed.

The Elim hymnal is called *Maran Ata*. It comes from Norway in a version with notes and one without notes and consists largely of translations of English and American gospel songs. Ebenezer uses a songbook called *Shibbolet* which comes only without notes. The songs were all composed by the Norwegian founder of the Free Friends. The lyrics of these songs, of which there are hundreds, dwell heavily on the dreadfulness of sin and the merits of the Blood and are set to sing-song tunes that all sound more or less alike, as they would have to be since they are never written down.

At the time of which I write my father is friendly to the people from Elim although he is an elder at Ebenezer. As an elder he prefers to keep his opinions to himself and let others lead. Yet on weighty matters he is consulted.

My father is night porter on Wall Street at the Guaranty Trust Company where he earns thirty-five dollars a week. Without drink, thirty-five dollars a week equals safety, respectability, happiness. Five dollars toward the rent, five dollars in the savings bank, fifteen dollars for the running of the household, and ten dollars left for tithes, small outings, packages for the relatives in Norway, sneakers in the summer, a second-hand mackinaw in the winter, such occasional capital expenditures as the cost of a used rug or sofa. A thousand calculations and it all fits as though by magic. With drink, all these things evaporate by the same inexorable arithmetic. My father in his view is a rich and lucky man.

My father has compassion for the bums that goes back to his own days as a sailor adrift in New York. The bums sleep in our vestibule sometimes and wet themselves and leave smelly puddles. My father takes them in the morning to the White Hut to see that they eat a hamburger and drink a cup of coffee. He won't give them the twenty cents because they would spend it on drink. In the early days he brought them into the house and gave them clean socks or a shirt, but my mother put a stop to that.

And so my father takes my brother and me to the various missions. Besides the Blue Cross, there is the Carroll Street Mission in South Brooklyn, the Norwegian Salvation Army at Fifth Avenue and 52nd Street, the Hospital and Prison

Mission, where Elim used to be. He thinks it is good for the bums to see some children. Perhaps to see the fruits of sobriety. But mainly because he knows they are lonely. He gets us to recite for them, long after Christmas is past, the pieces we learned for the Sunday school Christmas program at Ebenezer.

My father's peripatetic piety includes not only the missions but other churches and tabernacles, some far afield, in Elizabeth, in West New York, on Staten Island—all of which require hours of buses and ferries and buses again—several churches in Manhattan which are reached by subway, a place in Park Slope where a renegade group from Elim calling themselves The Latter Rain anoint one another apostles and prophets and speak ecstatically of Last Things. My father is intellectually restless. Not himself a learned man, or a man of prophetic calling, he has immense respect for men who open the divine mysteries, whose speech is authoritative, knotty, pregnant with import, full of hard sayings and precise calculation, whose words are long trajectories of casuistry spiced with irony and weighted with scriptural references. He sits, always in the rear of the hall, with a half-smile compounded of distraction and concentration, never really part of the doings about him, the only sign of his close attendance on the matter in hand a meticulous high-lighting of the opened scripture texts in red and blue pencils in his big Scofield Reference Bible.

Brother Bringsrud, whom my father comes to hear at the Blue Cross Mission, is a carpenter by trade. He owns a roomy Plymouth car in which he hauls variously the equipment of his trade, the songbooks and pump organ for street meetings, and the sisters who attend the Blue Cross. Brother Bringsrud is married to a stern and ugly woman who has the spiritual gift of discernment. Sister Bringsrud is usually elsewhere as a consequence, often with the Latter Rain people in Park Slope where she regularly discerns carnal manifestations in the exercise of more exuberant spiritual gifts than hers, and sometimes the influence of demons.

Brother Bringsrud builds houses on Long Island when the weather is good. He works alone, digging foundations by hand, cutting studs by hand too, eight or ten at a time with economical and powerful strokes of a beautifully oiled panel saw that serves also as a musical instrument. Brother Bringsrud keeps the saw always by him, in an oilskin case with a zipper along the back and two handles like those on a small valise. In the case, besides the precious saw, is a violin bow, a cake of rosin and a square of blue flannel cloth.

When Brother Bringsrud is about to play the saw he sits well forward on a chair, removes the cloth from the case and places it with nice adjustments over his left leg. Then the saw is taken up and the handle tucked under his thigh. Brother Bringsrud always pauses at this point to apply rosin to the bow, slowly, with prodigious care, like a woodcarver sharpening his chisels, as though in just this procedure lies the secret of his art. This done and the rosin stowed Brother Bringrud grasps the narrow end of the saw delicately but firmly with the left hand, bending the blade in a long arc downward over the cloth-covered leg and at the same time re-curving the tip upward with the fingers. As he plays, his right arm reaches across his body drawing the bow up and down on the smooth edge of the saw. The sound is an eerie, fragile, crystalline overtone, like a glass rubbed with a wet finger, a sound of pure timbre and indeterminate octave, a tone both clean and unclean. Pitch and volume are varied by the placement of the bow along the length of the saw and by subtle alterations in the elevation and curvature of the blade under Brother Bringsrud's strong fingers. An intermittent trembling of the right leg produces an expressive vibrato toward the end of long-held notes. Brother Bringsrud strokes the notes rather as an oarsman urges his boat along. He leans into the pull and then subsides, the bow delicately poised above the vibrating saw, then leans into the pull again, and again subsides, sometimes slowly, sometimes quickly.

Brother Bringsrud plays only when there is a request that touches him. He resists these requests unless he feels an anointing or feels a particular piece of music laid on his heart. He is often asked to play but often refuses.

Special music at the Blue Cross mission also consists of

duets from Sister Doris and Sister Sara. Sister Doris is plain and forthright. She had a husband but lost him to drink and another woman, and has raised two large unprepossessing boys on her own. She sings the low parts and strums a large guitar with a wide fretboard and a wide embroidered shoulder strap. Sister Sara has a high voice with a hint of some training, a tiny waist, yellow, softly-waved hair worn shoulder-length, Marlene Dietrich bones, pretty gold teeth that flash when she sings and a big hat. Behind her back Sister Sara is called Sara-with-the-hat-on. She has never married, a fact which excites pity among the sisters. Sister Doris and Sister Sara sing mostly the songs from *Shibbolet*. Sister Sara smiles and shuts her eyes and weaves her head in perfect sympathy with the dreadful sentiments of the numerous verses and lusty refrains.

Brother Bringsrud preaches in Norwegian, in deep and hearty chest tones and rolled r's. He is a florid man with unruly sand-coloured hair. He uses the trick of speaking on an intake of breath to good effect, ironic or droll according to his intention. Brother Bringsrud is also given to pious ejaculations uttered with a violence that arouses the bums from their torpor and sets off a chain of sympathetic exhalations from his hearers. A particularly explosive "Praise God!" "Thanks and Worship!" (a phrase of his own invention) brings Sister Sara to her feet, her eyes closed, her hands open in supplication. "Shun da mo sai!" she says with a delicate judder. Sometimes there is no more and Sister Sara subsides slowly into her seat.

Other times there is more. Then there is a pause, during which everyone closes their eyes. If the tongues goes on for a while, a decent interval is left afterwards to see whether there is an interpretation.

An interpretation is much less solemn than a prophecy, and not so rare. Prophecies happen at the Latter Rain meetings where there are people with the gift of prophecy. At the Blue Cross an interpretation is likely to come from Brother Bringsrud himself, which raises an issue of delicacy, because although it is known that Brother Bringsrud has the gift of interpretation, the message is in its nature a rebuke to those not attending in their hearts to the burden of Brother Bringsrud's sermon. Everyone knows, however, that the message is not his but Sister Sara's. He only interprets it, and is not deeply affected but can continue with his sermon where he left off, while Sister Sara continues visibly shaken during the interpretation and cries quietly for long after. Her distress is even greater when she has delivered a message in tongues and there is no interpretation. This is no reflection on Sister Sara since she has only the gift of tongues, but it is painful to see her holding her sides and rocking to and fro with something inside her that hasn't been released yet. At such times Brother Bringsrud goes very white and grim and when he returns to his sermon gets angrier or else he stops altogether and calls for a season of prayer.

The themes of Brother Bringsrud's sermons are two. One of them is the great apostasy of the churches. The other is the doctrine of the Last Days, a mighty and intricate theme woven out of the most obdurate and scattered texts in Scripture as though too awful to be laid right out in the open.

The first of these themes, the backsliding of the churches, is dwelt on as much in sorrow as in anger, and puts everyone in mind of Elim, although Elim is not actually mentioned. Brother Bringsrud is not openly critical of Elim because in a way its backsliding and worldliness (connected in some minds with the move from the old movie house into the gold and *faux marbre* opulence of the former Jewish Temple) opens a niche for his own prophetic talents.

A deeper source of Brother Bringsrud's feelings about Elim is his old rivalry with Pastor Finn Moe, which goes back to the days when there was only Ebenezer. Some people started Elim up in 1926—that was at the time the folk from Siloa, which used to be where Blue Cross is, joined with Ebenezer but weren't happy with the way Brother Bringsrud and his wife ran things and issued a call to Moe from Norway to be their pastor. Of course at the time of which I speak Pastor Moe is not even in Brooklyn but in Chicago. Arne Larsen is pastor in Elim and has been since the power struggle (just before the war, after Pastor Moe left Elim) that opened up the purchase of the Jewish Temple. But Pastor Moe's presence hovers over the Brooklyn churches and nowhere more than in Brother Bringsrud's mind.

For one thing Moe is an educated man. He holds a diploma from a technical course he took in Norway. More importantly, he regards himself as the protegé of the great Thomas Ball Barratt, the English-born founder and pastor of the Filadelfia Church in Oslo, whom the Free Friends resent because of the high-handed way he treated their own founder, Erik Andersen Nordquelle, the inspired poet of the *Shibbolet* verses. Only a few people in Elim know that Pastor Moe aspires to Pastor Barratt's pulpit. But Brother Bringsrud knows what some of even those few don't know, that Pastor Moe will never have the pulpit of Filadelfia Church. There are many other pretenders, and in spite of the fact that Pastor Moe let Pastor Barratt's sister Mary Ball "hide out" so to speak in Elim after the business with the deaconesses, there is the mess in Drammen from during the war when Pastor Moe found himself marooned in Norway.

The episode is obscure and people in Norway only cluck and raise their eyebrows about it and look as though they would rather forget it. What is certain is that Pastor Moe went over for a time to the Free Friends in Drammen and taught some simple people there that he was the Child in the Wilderness, and then went back over to the Filadelfia people when he had thought more about it and it seemed the war would end after all. My cousin Eva, who was a young girl in the Free Friends at the time, says that Pastor Moe is "not a nice man" and then purses her lips and will say no more. It is perhaps because of this history that Pastor Moe is not keen on Last Things and preaches instead in Chicago on the Deeper Life, which he has gotten from "The Christian's Secret of a Happy Life," a book by an Englishwoman that influenced the great Pastor Barratt and brought him out of a depression.

All this weighs heavily on Brother Bringsrud. He knows that he is jealous and tempted by spiteful feelings and prays often about it. For like my father he is respectful of the anointing of God which often falls on unlikely candidates.

My father speculates about this, the workings of the Spirit with His anointed servants being much in his thoughts. He talks such issues over with his friend Torvald Torvaldsen, who works at the bank where my father works and is also an elder at Ebenezer. My brother and I hear them late at night from our bunkbeds just next to the dining room. My father is persuaded that Brother Bringsrud has the interpretation to Sara's messages in tongues, but perhaps thinks it is too much for the others to bear and that it is up to him whether to keep it to himself or not, and that anyway he sometimes works the message into his sermon. My father further adduces places in the Bible where godly men actually quarrel with God and don't do what God wants, at least not immediately, and then sometimes win their argument and God changes his mind.

Or, what if Pastor Moe is indeed the Child and Brother Bringsrud knows it, from the tongues messages delivered by

Sister Sara that Brother Bringsrud will not interpret? Brother Torvaldsen, a tall morose man with a bald head and a disposition to clear and simple rules, thinks that interpretation is interpretation and you should deliver it as soon as you get it.

But this is an old argument that will get nowhere. These are matters for the Lord, and my father and Brother Torvaldsen always conclude these discussions by agreeing that people shouldn't put themselves forward too much.

Solveig

Since the operation Solveig had been studying herself in the full-length mirror behind her closet door with a new and detached interest. Dressings had given way to red crusted gashes and angry puckered flesh and this in turn to a settled topography whose contours she traced endlessly with her finger. Wide white tracks high under the arms, two long scallops where her breasts had been. Crooked, clumsy cuttings. A child's havoc. The thought brought a smile to her face.

The face was squarish and handsome, with wide cheekbones, a small upturned nose and a firm neck and chin. Her hair was still darkish blonde and thick and she took pains with it, plaiting it into a coil on top of her head just as she had in Berlin during the war. All that was a blur now, the victim of too many years of willed forgetfulness. And now more recently of another, puzzling forgetfulness that she sometimes tried to push back but sometimes surrendered to.

She found stockings and pulled them on, mildly surprised

at her clarity of mind. It occurred to her that Karl usually did this for her. At the back of the closet, behind the housecoats and dressing gowns, she found a grey wool dress that had not fitted her for many years but probably would now. She pulled the dress over her head and looked at herself in the mirror with a grave and critical intensity, turning this way and that and feeling the welcome prickling of vanity.

She had been full-breasted and had liked the way her cleavage showed. The expensive brassieres were still carefully laid away in tissue in the bottom drawer of her dressing table. The grey dress sagged at the top and the low neckline when she bent forward showed the whole of her devastated chest. She experimented like this several times and decided it didn't matter.

Karl was out on a job. He sanded floors and shampooed carpets, working alone with his heavy equipment. He didn't need to do this. They had sold the business many years before and moved to a place in the Poconos, but Karl was restless in retirement. Karl didn't read or talk to people, and when he had run out of improvements to make to their house (it was in any case new and didn't need improvements) he came to hate the Poconos. They moved back to Brooklyn to a ground-floor apartment in a duplex house near Eighth Avenue. A little bit at a time Karl had built up another business.

Karl was devoted to her and indulged her taste for pretty things. All her treasures had gone with them to the Poconos and most of them remained there in storage. It was a fiction between them that they were any day now going to retrieve the things from the Poconos but neither of them really wanted to. Karl liked the clean expanses of hardwood floor. He waxed and buffed all the rooms every week with his big machine. Solveig loved the openness and the way the light when the sun was out came through the blinds and made golden patterns on the polished floor. When she could she walked from room to room, listening to the echo of her feet. She knew that she would die here and that before she died her mind would slowly empty itself until it was like the apartment.

She went and sat in the living room, which looked out on the street. She looked at the patchy bark of the plane tree in front of the window. She saw heads going by, just visible above the sill. One went by quickly. Then for a long time nothing. Then another whose pauses and dips and sudden lunges argued irresistibly a leash and a large dog. She had become infinitely patient, a woman who had once been perpetually busy and brisk, who secretly relished her own irritability and quick mood changes.

She had had power over men, and having exercised it when she was young, she had grown bored with it. In any case she had had to survive, which was more interesting. She turned this over slowly, fusing the thought with the patchy bark. First there was Eirik. Little Eirik, not little any more, and far away somewhere. Then others later. She had been fierce over them. A tyrant of a mother, unappeasable, unreasonable.

Eirik's father had disappeared almost at once. He had a bland, oval boy's face with a small nose in the centre and a sensual mouth running to cruelty. He was big, faintly repulsive in his nudity like a large hairless baby, yet surprisingly supple and coordinated in his movements. He had toughened himself with exercises and weights and he crushed her will when he lay on her. He was a sailor and the first time he went away he had left her pregnant with his child.

Eirik grew to have something of his father's face, but he was slender and vulnerable; he had shivered constantly as a little boy, even when it wasn't cold. In this boy she discovered her fate and she bound herself to him.

Later, in New York, Solveig met Karl, who was also a sailor. He drank and had other women and sometimes hit her, but he was away a lot of the time. She had more children, Liv and Greta and little Tom. Eventually Karl tired of the sea and of his rages and found the Lord. Onkel Ole and Tante Aase said it was in answer to their prayers, and perhaps it was. He became a good provider and at last the indignities were over. Yet none of this touched the core of her fantasy, that Eirik was the man of the house. She identified him in her mind with her father.

Solveig's father had always known what to do. Even in the war, Peter Nordhus had kept a level head. He kept orders coming in for his boats. He suffered no nonsense from his employees and he saved their jobs for them, to small thanks afterwards it must be said. He could see signs of trouble, with a house full of daughters and the German barracks just down by the river where the girls liked to walk in the evening. It was only a matter of time before Solveig, who was high-spirited and well-developed, would bring ruin down on them.

Nordhus had connections with the better sort of Germans and when the chance came to send Solveig away he took it. The district procurement officer for the Wehrmacht, a decent fellow named Keller, who had discreetly put in his way some business of a civil rather than military sort, told him that Solveig could find safe work at a respectable club in Berlin, and assured him that some connections of his would keep an eye on her.

In Norway afterwards it was difficult to explain things. A madness seized everyone, as though they had forgotten how one had had to survive and how uncertain things had been. Nordhus's accounts were gone through by the commission on collaboration. It came to nothing, but the boat business languished for a time. The family was in a hard way, and it had become impossible for Solveig in the close and poisonous atmosphere of Drammen. She went to Oslo and worked as a typist, sending some of her small earnings home. There she met Eirik's father and was soon pregnant. Before Eirik reached his first birthday it was clear she was going to be on her own. Her mother Signe arranged with Onkel Ole to sponsor Solveig in

America, and raised the money to send Solveig and Eirik to New York to start a new life. Solveig never believed her father was behind this scheme, or would have permitted it if he had been himself and had not been hounded by difficulties.

Solveig suddenly remembered the time. She would have to make coffee. She went to the kitchen and got out the percolator and set it going. She hunted up the silver service, still in a cardboard box from the move. It needed polishing but it would have to do now. She got out some cream and some cubes of sugar and put these in the little silver pitcher and the sugar bowl with the small silver tongs, and brought these things to the living room and set them on the bare coffee table, which, with a beige armchair and a beige sofa, was all the room contained. She made one more trip for the cups and saucers and the little spoons and some napkins and brought these to the coffee table. It was now two o'clock. Almost immediately the door bell rang and she got up to let Tante Edith in.

It was strange to think of Tante Edith as belonging to the generation of her parents and Onkel Ole and Tante Aase, who were all dead now. Tante Aase wasn't really her aunt. She had been a girlhood friend of Solveig's mother Signe. They had been in the Free Friends meeting in Arendal together, and Tante Aase had married the son of the banker Aardal. Martin Aardal had been disowned for joining the Free Friends, and so in 1923 they came together to America. Tante Aase had stayed in touch with her old friend and when Signe's younger brother Ole came to New York, Signe asked her to look out for him. Aase was glad when Ole found the Lord and decided he was ready to settle down and take a wife, but she didn't think much of Tante Edith, who was too young and not Norwegian.

Onkel Ole had died long ago. Tante Aase had lived until just last year and had left Solveig her copy of *Shibbolet*, the songbook of the Free Friends. Solveig had the copy rebound in leather and the words "Aase Aardal" stamped in gold on the cover. It lay in front of her on the coffee table where she had kept it since the funeral.

Solveig's face was composed, her mouth set in a soft smile. She was thinking it was important to remember everything, for once to be absolutely present to something that happened to her. Tante Edith, she could see, was nervous. Her eyes avoided Solveig altogether, because there was nowhere to look except at the place where there should have been a prosthesis. The absence under Solveig's dress deprived Tante Edith of the word, which she would have savoured to herself, as she did all words having to do with disease and surgery. She was also nervous about something happening. She knew about Solveig's lapses and about how wonderful Karl was about it all, a real saint, and not many men would do it, what with the toilet and getting her dressed and all. Tante Edith inquired with seeming nonchalance about where Karl was, and fidgeted anxiously when she learned he would not be back until evening. Tante Edith gabbled about grandchildren and fished out pictures. Pimply, delinquent-looking older ones, already making babies themselves, then some younger ones with thick dark hair and bright animal eyes.

Solveig looked on with feigned interest. When she could she studied the other woman in the afternoon light. Tante Edith was scarcely older than Solveig. Time had erased what there was of the older woman's seniority. It had as well, Solveig realized with a sudden fierce pride, been kinder to Solveig, for all her ruined body and deteriorating mind. Tante Edith's clothes were shapeless and had no style. The skirt was too short and rode up in the front on a swollen belly. There were spots on the front of her blouse that no one had tried to remove. She wore no make-up or earrings. The sallow face with its large pores were waxy with neglect, and her black hair was lifeless. The words Tante Edith spoke were a stream of clichés, and platitudes garnered from oceans of church. Behind it all, in the bottomless liquid of Tante Edith's chocolate brown eyes, a need, a great unconsoled baby's need. Solveig fought back the tears that wanted to come. She saw herself in danger of being cheated, not of revenge, much less of forgiveness, but of being heard.

"You have brought something," Solveig said in an interval in the flow, nodding slightly toward the white box tied with string that Tante Edith had put on the coffee table between them. "You shouldn't have. But you see how it is. We are not settled. I meant to go out this morning to get something."

"Well, I wouldn't expect you to do that," Tante Edith said eagerly and too quickly, and frightened herself.

Solveig took the box to the kitchen and put the pastries that were in it on little plates. She put forks on the plates and napkins and carried them back to the living room. She let Tante Edith begin eating her pastry. She didn't touch her own, but looked out the window at the patched bark, now golden along one side from the late afternoon sun.

"Edith," she began, using perhaps for the first time the woman's name by itself, "it is good that you came today. Since your call I have been thinking of some things I have to say to you." Solveig hesitated. This had already cost her nearly all of her energy. At last she said quietly, "I had for many years a resentment toward you." Tante Edith began to make little mewling noises of protest, not knowing whether she was going to be accused of something or hear a confession, and equally frightened of both. Her mouth had the bitter twist of someone who has endured every abuse and misunderstanding, enough for a lifetime, for many lifetimes. The liquid brown eyes, however, were pleading. She had done nothing wrong in her whole life. No amount of experience had ever prepared her for the crazy things people would say next. She looked as though she wanted to stop her ears and howl, before the thing, whatever it was, came out and couldn't be put back again.

Solveig waited, refusing to be hurried. While she waited she thought of the day she stepped off *Stavangerfjord* with Eirik, who immediately burst into tears at the sight of a black man on the pier. *Svart mann, mama* he wailed over and over. Onkel Ole was also on the pier. She recognized her mother's features in him at once, and was reassured by the Norwegian greeting and the formal manners, which did not seem cold but firm and solid and something you could trust. The younger of Onkel Ole's two boys had come along. She recognized him from the pictures, but was not prepared for how un-Norwegian he looked, the first of many small disorienting perceptions about this new life.

Onkel Ole had come on the subway and apparently expected to go back the same way. When he saw what a large trunk she had and that he would have to hire a taxi he became angry. She could see his jaw tremble and knew that he was thinking it was her stupidity that put him in this situation. The ride to Brooklyn was a nightmare. She tried to keep from crying and make everything worse. She had the first intimation of what an awful thing she must have done when the taxi driver at first didn't want to take them at all, and then the trip was so long, over a bridge and along interminable avenues, and Onkel Ole staring at the amount on the meter. When at last they arrived Onkel Ole had to go in to get money. She knew later that this would have come out of the jar with Tante Edith's household money in it and that there would have been words, first disbelieving and then bitter, as there always was about anything that happened that wasn't expected. Her first view of Tante Edith, as Solveig sat in the taxi waiting for Onkel Ole to return, feeling utter shame and wishing she were dead, was a scowling face at the door briefly when Onkel Ole emerged with some paper money in his hand.

Somehow Solveig had got through the day. Tante Edith had baked a cake and made coffee, and tried to make her feel welcome, and Tante Aase came over to see her. Tante Aase turned out to be a bossy, well-meaning, keen-eyed woman. She sniffed disapprovingly at the cake, an American-style thing with icing made of margarine. Solveig instantly liked her.

Solveig was to stay with Onkel Ole and Tante Edith while she got on her feet. Their flat was long and narrow and occupied the ground floor of a three-storey frame house. There were four rooms directly in a line from front to back. The living room looked out on the street. Immediately behind it and separated only by a pair of sliding doors with frosted glass, which were usually open, was Onkel Ole and Tante Edith's bedroom. Then there was a tiny room in which the two boys slept in bunk-beds. Last was a dining room which looked out on the back yard. To the side of the dining room was a small kitchen that also looked out on the back and a windowless bathroom shared by the whole family. In the kitchen Onkel Ole had installed a crude door where the window had been and outside this window had built a porch of crumbly cement. The back yard had grass and was shaded by a big tree and made a pleasant retreat in good weather and a place for Eirik to play.

The only place for Solveig and Eirik was the fold-out sofa in the living room, which was also the only place for the family to sit or entertain during the day. Every night, Solveig had to make up a bed after Onkel Ole and Tante Edith had retired and had closed the sliding doors, which nevertheless concealed little because of the frosted glass. She undressed in the dark, and had to perform her toilet and take Eirik to the bathroom if he woke in the night by opening the door into the outer hall, locking it behind her with the skeleton key, tiptoeing down the hall to the back entrance to the flat, letting herself in with another key, using the toilet as quietly as she could, and then doing it all again in reverse to get back to bed. On the rare occasions that she came in late she would have to let herself in the back way and try to get through the dining room, the boys' room, and Onkel Ole and Tante Edith's bedroom without waking anyone.

In all this she struggled with Tante Edith's passive but implacable resentment. She didn't dare invite men or even speak of men she met from time to time. She stopped using lipstick, because they didn't approve of this in the church where Onkel Ole and Tante Edith went, and where she and Eirik went too, out of prudence and also out of loneliness. Solveig found it comforting to see Tante Aase, who also went to their church but refused to be a member because the Free Friends didn't believe in memberships. She liked Tante Aase's oddities and prejudices and that she made Tante Edith nervous whenever she visited.

You gave me one drawer to put our things in. Me and Eirik. Just one drawer.

That was it, what she had had to say. It didn't sound like much, now it was out, the words Solveig had turned over and over with wonder for so long. She was not even sure now whether she had said it out loud or only to herself. She felt dreadfully tired.

The front door opened and she heard Karl dragging his machine up over the step.

Tante Edith heard this as well and could not disguise her relief. "Hello Karl," she called. "Working hard?"

"Hardly working, Edith," came the expected response. They both laughed appreciatively.

Tante Edith stood. She turned to Solveig and said how wonderful the day had been and how good the coffee and that Solveig was not to think about the old days which had been so hard but to have hope in the future and that she was so lucky to have Karl.

Tante Edith turned to Karl as she started for the door. "It is wonderful the way you are managing. I don't know how you do it."

Tante Edith had reached the shore of safety.

Solveig looked down at Tante Aase's copy of *Shibbolet*. She picked it up and held it to the wound of her bosom. She turned her back on them and walked out of the room, her feet echoing on the bare wooden floors. She could hear their whispers as she shut her bedroom door.

Old Photos

The scene is a bar or cabaret. Four women with marcelled hair and powdered faces entertain two men at a table. The wall against which the table is placed is occupied with a large mirror, in which unseen lights leave spots of glare. Reflected also in the mirror is the litter of bottles, glasses and ash-trays on the table. The photograph is brightly lit, grainy, slightly askew. The effect of the scene, without doubt intended by the photographer, is a feeling of oppression and unease.

One of the men is turned slightly away from the camera. His face is further obscured by a hand holding a cigarette. He is attending to the woman on his right.

The other man is sitting opposite the first, his back to the camera. His face, however, is reflected in the mirror.

The man in the mirror is young, in his twenties. He is slight and fair with a high forehead and a face that narrows toward the chin. His ears stand out from his head. He wears a hat, rather than a cap, pushed back. His reflected image is looking directly into the camera, but the gaze is uncomprehending. The man is drunk. His arms are around the women on either side of him, awkwardly, the boldness of the gesture not concealing his inexperience. His eyes are wide open, disbelieving, startled by something more than the bright lights. Their paleness in the photograph suggests blue eyes, Northern eyes.

The face of the man in the mirror is the face of my father.

I am sure of this even though there are difficulties with the dates. The caption in the book of photographs says that this picture was taken in Paris about 1926, at a bar frequented by foreign seamen. My father was supposed to have been settled in America by 1920, but he might have gone to France later. He had certainly been there before.

The only other bit of evidence with a bearing on this matter is a seaman's document of my father's, dated July, 1920 in New York. On the back he scrawled a name and an address in St. Denis. I cannot decipher the last name, but the first is unmistakably "Arthur." In any event I think of the Arthur of the document as the same man as the other man in the photograph, the one across the table whose features are obscured. Furthermore, I connect this Arthur with a man I remember from an episode in my childhood.

Thanksgiving Day in New York is often chill and windy. It was the one day of the year that was like Sunday, but without church. Everything about the day had an uneasy quality. It was the custom in the neighbourhood for children to go out begging in the morning. You rang doorbells and said "Anything for Thanksgiving." People shoved oranges and walnuts at you, and on the street night-workers coming up from the subway gave you pennies. However, my brother and I were forbidden to beg. Our mother thought such things common. Instead, while she prepared the turkey or the ham for Thanksgiving dinner, my father took my brother and me for a walk.

My brother is still in short pants and I am in a knickerbockers suit with long socks. Both of us wear mackinaws with zippered hoods. My father has on his best hat: pearl-grey with a wide slate-coloured band and a tiny feather. He rolls from side to side when he walks, like a ship in heavy weather.

We do not talk on these walks, or play, even if we go to Sunset Park or Bliss Park or Leif Eriksson Square, because we have our best clothes on. Anyway the parks are empty of human life. Sheets of old newspapers spin in the wind, which also blows grit into our eyes. Fingers freeze to the monkey bars, and the boards of the seesaws have been removed.

More often on these occasions we walk down to the docks through the deserted holiday streets: across Fourth Avenue, down the last steep stretch of Bay Ridge brownstones, past Third Avenue and the overhead train and the flop houses, to the forbidden zone beyond.

You can't get really close to the water down here, but the

smells of tide and tar and bird droppings are strong, and also the smell of the garbage in the scows at the Sanitation Department pier at 52nd Street. Piers and warehouses and freight yards have taken over a once densely populated district of dock-workers and their families, although a few mean houses persist on the side streets, and saloons still cling to the corners. We pass catwalks arching over oil-soaked tracks, vacant lots of brown weeds and broken glass, stacks of crates behind chain link fences, cranes and shunting engines and other machinery. A watchman sits staring at nothing, as though blind, in his booth by a warehouse gate.

My father explains nothing and looks at nothing and his pace is uncomfortable for us. Rather than lag behind we run on ahead. "Run on ahead," he says. "Wait at the corner." Or at the tracks. Or at the gas tank. And so we tear away pell-mell, arms pumping, to loiter at the designated place for my father to catch up. I experimentally apply arm and head locks to my brother while he half-heartedly kicks me in the leg, both of us watching for my father's rolling windward approach, hat down by his ears, hands thrust deep in his overcoat pockets, his blue eyes far away.

On these walks to the docks we always stop to see Arthur. (I have, as you see, come to call him this, although I have no clear memory of a name for him then.)

Arthur's feet swell badly. One shoe is cut open down to the toe. He is fat and breathes noisily with every movement.

His room, at the top floor of a brownstone near Third Avenue, lies part way along the landing and has no outside window. A little light filters in from an air well. He has a narrow cot and a few possessions on shelves, hooks to hang his clothes on, and a single chair. There is a toilet with a brown wooden seat and a pull-chain in a closet off the landing.

During these visits my brother and I stand awkwardly in the little room or wander out to the landing and hang over the banister. My father and Arthur murmur in Norwegian, a lulling sing-song on topics forever lost.

When we are ready to leave Arthur presses on my father an evaporated milk tin with a slot punched in the top with a knife blade, in which he has put pennies during the year, for the missionary offering at Sunday school, where my mother is superintendent of the cradle roll and the children's department. My father takes the heavy tin without comment and puts it in a paper bag he has brought for this purpose. Later, my mother will open it with a can-opener and wash the sour-smelling pennies before counting them and twisting them into papers, fifty to a roll, to take to Sunday School. My mother makes wry faces during this operation because Arthur is not a Christian and shows no signs of becoming one, and because it was a principle governing life in the city that you never knew where things had been and coins in particular.

On one of these Thanksgivings, when he had already taken the evaporated milk tin with the pennies and put it in the paper bag, my father, on an impulse, invited Arthur to come along for dinner.

Arthur arrived late. My mother was angry and then sullen and the meal went badly. My father made it worse. He made my brother and me recite our Sunday-school Christmas pieces, even though we had just got them and didn't know them very well yet. Then we had to sing our Sunday-school songs for Arthur, "Climb, climb up sunshine mountain," and then "Jesus loves the little children" in Chinese, which we had learned from Sister Sorlie who had been a missionary in China and whose face was scarred by smallpox.

We had to stand close to Arthur during this recitation and we could smell his clothes and wanted to pull away and my father got red in the face and gave us angry looks.

My father announced after a time that he was walking Arthur back to his room, and I was to go along. I didn't want to go, and my mother gave him looks, but he insisted, perhaps as some sort of punishment of her, or of me. There was no way to tell.

It had got colder since the morning and Arthur could not walk very well, but instead of going to his room we went to Sunset Park, at the top of the ridge overlooking the harbour.

They walked side by side in the clear autumnal light, my father walking more slowly than usual, in consideration of Arthur, who was pitched forward and shuffling in his clumsy shoe, with obvious difficulty and pain, against the sharp wind.

We walked across the park to the edge of the long hill that sweeps down to the bay, from where we could see the ships and the Statue of Liberty sharp and clear and tiny. The deep ultramarine of the water faded to pale green at the foot of the Battery and toward New Jersey. Everywhere the water was agitated by the wind into flecks of white that flashed tiny and quick on the surface. Cirrus clouds high above Manhattan raced toward the Sound, making the earth seem to move beneath our feet.

Arthur's face was blue and veined like a cheese. A drop of clear mucus hung on the end of his nose. He glanced at me and then at my father. My father turned away but I could see his jaw tremble and the muscles working just below his ear. I knew he was very angry, and that it had to do with Arthur. I sensed, even then, in a child's first intimation of the intricate passions of adult life, that their quarrel, if that is what to call something so silent and awful, had nothing to do with the unhappy day, but was ancient, and deeper than words. I wanted to howl in misery from fear and the cold but didn't dare, and stood back and kept quiet until they were at last ready to move off, over the brow of the hill and homeward.

So far as I know my father never saw Arthur again after that day. His name was never mentioned in our house that I recall, and my father has been dead for many years. I saw Arthur again, however, in a quite unexpected way.

Gustav Løvland, or Brother Løvland—we called everyone connected with the church Brother and Sister in those days— was a house-painter by trade and later custodian at Sailor's Snug Harbor, on Staten Island, where a dwindling handful of sailing-ship veterans shuffled about among enormous rosewood billiard tables and ship models in glass cases. Although Brother Løvland lived in this modest way, his brother had been a minister of the crown in Norway. That was the way things were with Norwegians in Brooklyn.

Brother Løvland was a fine musician and respected as a man of culture and of lofty character. He played the violin and in the twenties had written music, gospel songs with verses and a refrain, and published them on sheets with his photograph on the cover, a lean aristocratic face and a wild mane of hair.

I courted his daughter Ingrid, who was thin and sweet and wore kerchiefs on her head in the manner of those days. This courting required stamina: a long walk from 53rd Street to the Staten Island Ferry terminal, the passage on the ferry, the bus from St. George to Clove Lake Park, the hike across the park to the Løvlands, and then back again in the early hours of the morning.

Brother Løvland had a man he called Tafts to dinner one night, an untidy hulk of a man with dreadfully wheezing lungs and swollen feet. This was my Arthur, the Arthur of the Thanksgiving dinner and the sour pennies.

I am certain he didn't recognize me, and I said nothing. After dinner Tafts consented to play the piano, and launched on a Liszt Rhapsody which he played with reckless attack. He lifted his great fists high over his head and brought them crashing down in glancing hammer blows that ended far off the end of the keyboard. All this over his heavy breathing, and grunts of pain because of his feet.

The talk that evening was of Brahms and Schubert, punctuated by illustrative passages, played impetuously and argumentatively by Tafts on the piano with more wheezes and grunts, or meditatively and with modest authority by Brother Løvland on his violin, which he always kept by him.

Another world was opened to me, and I forgot Ingrid completely. After playing some other pieces on the piano Tafts launched into stories that kept us spellbound until much too late for me to catch my bus. I walked the several miles to St George and caught the ferry at dawn.

I never thought in those days to attempt to piece together any of these fragments into a history, or to ask anyone about them who might have known. The discovery of the photograph of my father in a cabaret in France, caused me to consider him in a wholly new light and gave me a motive for unravelling the mystery of Arthur. I became mildly obsessed with it, spending a good deal of time going through some old photos of my father's, which my mother gave me one day in a distracted and offhand mood.

I managed to identify here and there a picture I was rather sure was of Arthur and my father, most of them from the twenties, before my father found religion. In one they pose with other young men at a Coney Island bath house. Another shows them on a picnic, with a car. Arthur is lounging on the running board playing a guitar to two young women in slacks and head-bands who are preparing a lunch on a blanket. My father is sitting stiffly in the back seat of the car. In a third, my father stands on the deck of a ferry between two laughing women with heavy legs in shiny stockings and cloche hats. I imagine Arthur to be the photographer.

One set of images in the album I return to again and again. Three photographs. All taken about the same time. The scenes are in Norway. It must be about 1915 or 1916.

The first photograph shows two young men sitting on a log, one of whom is my father. The print has so faded that his nose is no more than two oily spots and his lips a faint pink line. He looks chubbier than he later became and his suit is ill-fitting and puckered at the seams. A boater is pushed to the back of his head. The eyes are round, pale, the pupils dark pinpoints. Arthur—it must be he—is slighter than my father. One leg is placed over the knee of the other. His boater is cocked forward and his eyes and much of his face are in shade.

The second picture is clearer than the first. A pretty girl is standing on wooden steps in front of a white building. Her dress is plain and hangs straight to just above her ankles. I imagine the dress to be dove-grey, or perhaps plum. She is wearing boots done up with hooks. She has no hat or gloves. Her hair is dark and piled loosely on her head and caught untidily in a ribbon. She is smiling. Her mouth is wide and her teeth regular and her eyes are full of merriment.

The last picture is of the white building, which appears to be a dormitory. The building is two storeys high and very wide with many windows. The door and the wooden steps on which the girl had been standing we can now see are at the centre of the building. There is a small x in blue ink on one of the upper-storey windows, the second one from the left.

As I have recently thought over these odd events and inscrutable images I am struck by the mystery and the sadness of the lives of the dead. What had happened to Arthur? What had happened to my father? Would this girl with the wide mouth and merry eyes have saved either of them?

I learned only recently, on a visit to a friend in Norway, what happened to Brother Løvland. There had been an accident, she said, many years ago, the death of a grandchild, a boy, Ingrid's child, one winter at Sailor's Snug Harbor. The boy had been left in the care of his grandfather. He slipped under the ice in the fountain pool and drowned before anything could be done. Brother Løvland blamed himself and died shortly afterwards of an inconsolable grief.

Brückenkopfstrasse

The house in Brückenkopfstrasse must have been very old, but it had no particular architectural character. There was scarcely any vantage point from which one might have formed an impression of the whole. There were not even any definite levels or storeys or a definite front and back. Small irregular windows were stuck here and there in the yellowish stucco, and gave no clue to the internal arrangements. One entered the house by a nondescript door in a narrow cul-de-sac off the street, which twisted on itself twice in the space of a hundred metres from where it began on the Handschuhsheim road until it petered out at the river bank, opposite and a bit downstream from the castle and the old city.

Inside the house, short irregular flights led up and round and off at odd angles to a series of apartments. There was only one water closet in the whole building and this was just inside the entrance, behind a primitive door of nailed boards open at top and bottom. A bathtub in the ancient catacomb under the house, whose hot water had to be heated for each bath by means of a briquette-fired boiler, completed the public amenities. Otherwise each flatlet had its own hodgepodge of lumpy and rickety furnishings and assorted, mostly dangerous, arrangements for heating and cooking and minor ablutions.

The landlady, Frau Kellermann, a widow who lived somewhere in the back parts of the premises, rented these accommodations at the most the market would bear with the minimum adherence to her obligation in law and morality, in the fixed belief that she was perpetually the victim of cheats, and in particular that the clapped-out furniture left for the use of each tenant, became, in the mere process of transfer from one tenant to the next, new and shining things unaccountably stained, broken down and worthless in no time. As most of her tenants were necessarily poor students, foreigners, people of irregular habits and schedules, her plaints had a racial tinge to them. She said of the Turks, for example—none of whom she had ever taken on as tenants, but of whom she had heard a great deal from her professional contacts with other landladies—that they were a very dirty people, and also that they were ruinous as tenants by dint of the quantities of hot water they used for their frequent baths.

She had somewhere got the mistaken idea that I understood her lengthy tirades in German. I thought it best to hear her out at these moments and nod occasionally, and from which harangues, by dint of frequent repetition of a few key words, I came to understand that Frau Kellermann regretted the passing of a more orderly time in the past, and looked with fading hope for a similar one in future. She disapproved of the proprietor of a tiny shop in our cul-de-sac, a Herr Schuler, who sold us eggs, candling them one at a time at an electric bulb embedded in the wall behind his counter, and wrapping each one separately in a twist of brown paper. Frau Kellermann said he had been an SS officer in the war. What she particularly disapproved of was that the war had permitted Herr Schuler to rise above his station.

In the year and a half I lived in Brückenkopfstrasse, with my first wife and our infant son, I was the only American soldier there. The other tenants included M. Martin, an aloof Frenchman who smelled of garlic, and who lived just inside the entrance, opposite the WC. A few steps up and to the left were a Guyanese student named Clement and his English wife Amanda. They had many interesting friends, including a homesick girl from Birmingham, whose accent they made fun of, who was desperate to get out of a condition of virtual slavery to a German baker she had promised to marry. The hapless girl had discovered that she was meant to be servant and drudge to her future mother-in-law, a bitter and resentful woman who did not like her son marrying a foreigner. The baker, when Amanda's Brummie friend told him she wanted to break off the engagement, insisted on holding her to the free labour he had counted on from a wife and thought he was entitled to, at least until he could find a replacement, and hid her passport and money as insurance against her flight. There were many tears over this in the flat, amid high-sounding expostulations from Clement, who was excitable, a communist, a supporter of the Guyana firebrand Cheddi Jagan, and anyway had a dim view of Germans. Clement was reading medicine, and his plan was to skip the lectures and read English medical books while swotting German, in hopes that these streams would come together in time for his examinations. In pre-1968 Europe you could do such things. Clement and I frequently went together for talks over potato soup at Mensa, the cheap student dining hall not far from the site of the old Heidelberg synagogue. Amanda, besides perpetually comforting her friend, minded our baby when my wife got ill and went to hospital.

At the top of the house, in the least salubrious spot, a garret really, lived a Hungarian medical student, Dezso Benyo, and his French wife, a poor mousy thing who spoke not a word of anything but French. This did not prevent her teaching my wife, similarly and stubbornly unilingual, to knit, which they did together at a furious pace. They evolved a voluble intercourse consisting mainly of shouting and pointing. Dezso, by contrast, spoke at least six languages fluently and, judging by his English, with colourful abandon. Dezso had been in every army there was during the war, switching sides as exigencies demanded or opportunity offered, and was lucky enough, or prescient enough, to end the war in an American uniform, and had thus acquired a US passport. He had an amazing command of GI obscenities with which he salted a continuous stream of Hungarian, Russian and German directed at the heads of the many students and émigrés who showed up at the numerous drunken parties in their tiny flat. I thought he was a spy and had been planted in Heidelberg by some espionage service to recruit agents. He in turn seemed to think of me as a hopeless naïf in regard to everything political, and greeted everything I said about America and the cold war with affectionate tolerance and of course complete disbelief. He was vastly amused at my aborted attempt to emigrate with my family to Australia. He was scornful of all deliberate self-improvement schemes, all bourgeois politics, all optimisms whatever. Dezso and his wife had a daughter, Madeleine, a fey pre-pubescent child dressed always in crisply starched costumes of delicate grey or mauve stripes, cut to an old-fashioned sailor-dress pattern, to which on Sundays was added a wide-brim straw with a long, trailing ribbon. Altogether a miracle of imagination and resistance on the part of Mme Benyo.

Then there was Gaby, the landlady's daughter. Baptized Gabriele, she had been married to an American army captain who had left Gaby with a son, a scruffy street-arab, about twelve years old, who ran errands for his grandmother and perhaps spied on the tenants for her too. Gaby was an indifferent mother. It was not clear where the boy slept, probably with his grandmother. You could see his sharp feral face peering around corners at unexpected times and places. Gaby spoke English and so relayed the more complicated complaints and instructions involving the running of the house, such as those having to do with blockage in the toilet or rubbish on the stairs, but it was her boy that tracked me down after I left Brückenkopfstrasse, with a message from his grandmother that the sofa in our flat, a broken-backed put-you-up on which several cycles of tenants had slept and ate and made love, was in worse condition than when we had got it, and demanding compensation.

Gaby kept one of the flats, just a room with a small kitchen, but the one with the best view. A skinny woman with bleached hair and a cheerful slap-dash manner, she had a lover, an Italian named Sergio who appeared and disappeared for periods of several days and sometimes weeks in his Alfa Romeo, smuggling various sorts of contraband in a small-time way between Germany and Italy. On occasion he left a parcel with us, little heavy things wrapped in brown paper and string which I hid in the toe of one my spit-shined parade boots until he called for whatever it was (I never asked or looked), and then he would leave a bottle of some sticky aperitif or other in gratitude for the favour. Frau Kellermann did not approve of Sergio, needless to say, and the Hungarian would have nothing to do with him, a thing to which I attributed a significance, and which perhaps had some influence on my decision in the case I am about to relate.

At the base where I worked as operations clerk in a military police unit, I sometimes relieved the desk sergeant at the entrance kiosk to the headquarters caserne. At the desk, which admitted hundreds of German workers every day, as well as top American brass, we employed a civilian translator named Müller, a smarmy fellow with a pock-marked face who engaged in a variety of petty extortions as a sideline or benefit of his go-between position, but who was tolerated nonetheless because he knew everybody and had a ferret's instinct for every sort of dodge and trick and underhandedness that presented itself.

One day, in a slack moment at the desk, Müller announced in his creepy way that he had something to show us boys, something really juicy.

Müller was an amateur photographer who had connections with all the photographic clubs and darkroom facilities around Heidelberg and did portraits and other custom work. He had a line of black-and-white postcard views of the castle and the bridge and so forth, all with nice dramatic cloud contrasts, done with filters, which he was happy to explain to you, that sold briskly to tourists.

He knew an Italian, Müller said, who had taken some pictures of his girlfriend, and had brought the film to Müller to develop. At first, Müller explained, the Italian only wanted them for himself. But he had been quickly talked into a joint venture with Müller, peddling additional prints to select customers, with the proviso—these being men of scruple—that the photos be cropped to conceal the subject's identity. The girlfriend was not to know about this bit of delicate traffic. Whereupon Müller handed round among the three or four of us working in the kiosk that day, samples of the photographs.

They were all of the same naked skinny blonde woman. There were none that showed the face of the model and there was no one else in any of the pictures. On one of these pictures I recognized the ring, a distinctive ring with a large lozenge-shaped stone that Gaby always wore on the middle finger of her right hand.

That afternoon I rang up a friend of mine in military intelligence named Barney.

Barney and I met before my wife came over from New York. I was living in the barracks, and got away as much as I could, trying, unsuccessfully, in my close-cropped hair and military-issue black shoes, to look inconspicuous at the cafés and recital halls and small galleries around Heidelberg, and even at the cellar clubs that featured apache dancers and camp reviews whose topical references and Berlin slang were quite beyond me. These clubs were frequented by refugees from the East, then mostly rootless young people, who had made it over the border in those days before the Wall. I met Barney in one of these places one night. We had similar cultural interests, and took to hanging out together. He had cultivated an appearance that allowed him to pass as European, buying his clothes and getting his hair cut in town, besides speaking excellent German. I eagerly took cues from his manners and the kinds of things he ordered to eat and drink.

Barney had managed to keep his homosexuality a secret from his superiors in the intelligence unit, whose work in Heidelberg was to keep an eye on the student right-wing clubs, and the numerous refugees from the communist East, and try to ignore the old Nazis clustered around the villa of the commander-in-chief up on the mountain. Gay men were of course in those days thought to be peculiarly vulnerable to blackmail, besides being a threat to morale generally. Barney would have been summarily dismissed from his position and from the Army had he been rumbled.

After my wife arrived he visited us often, never failing to bring a few bottles of good wine. He refused to drink the house favourite of Brückenkopfstrasse, a manufactured "Chianti" which was four marks, or one dollar, for a two-litre straw-wrapped bottle.

When I rang Barney that day from the desk sergeant's phone, we agreed to meet later in the enlisted men's club, and there I laid out the story of Gaby and Sergio and Müller and the ring. Barney said he would leak word in the right quarter about the suspicious activities of a certain Italian in an Alfa Romeo. However it came about, Sergio disappeared from Brückenkopfstrasse and Müller came for a while to wear a hunted look.

I did not see Gaby for a long time, until the day she invited everyone from Brückenkopfstrasse to the confirmation of her boy, who appeared at the church scrubbed and almost angelic. Besides his mother and grandmother, there were M. Martin, Dezso and Mme Benyo—and Madeleine, in a straw with a round crown and a longer ribbon than ever. My wife and I were there of course, and Amanda and her Brummy friend. Clement, true to his principles, would not set foot in a church. The Catholic service was offhand and hurried, but the two English women cried anyway.

When I saw how sad and thin Gaby was and how aged she had become in a short time, how altogether alone in the world she was, I had my first serious doubts about what I had done. I decided the Hungarian was probably right about me, and, for a time at least, swore off interfering in things I didn't understand.

Réfléchissez

I was discharged from the US Army in May, 1962, one month short of a three-year enlistment, having landed by troopship at the Army Port of Embarkation in Brooklyn, after an inconclusive skirmish with sea-sickness and a nine-day crap game on a gangway between decks all the way from Bremerhaven. From that queasy passage across the North Atlantic I remember few things in any detail. Among these is a certain black staff sergeant who, between rolls of the dice, defended the Furtwängler Beethoven recordings against the then-favourite Bruno Walter. The army was like that in those days: a cabinet of curiosities.

One of the things I realized in that next year, while working two jobs—a bank teller in Manhattan, a night shipping clerk in Queens—saving money for college and waiting for our second child to be born, was that I lacked any useful political ideas. I bought copies of The National Review and The New Republic and Commentary from a kiosk one morning in

Bryant Park and read them through on the subway between jobs. Before my train got me back to Brooklyn at 2:00 a.m. I was a Keynesian and a liberal. I took out subscriptions to The New Republic and Commentary, and then the TLS, and these more or less got me through the next few years.

I had some idea what I was getting into with this intellectual baggage when we moved the next summer to Springfield, Missouri. where I had nevertheless enrolled, on the basis of dubious advice and an itch for change, in a small liberal arts college operated by a white, conservative, Pentecostal denomination with headquarters in Springfield. The college was a raw new academy set up in a former military hospital. The buildings were asbestos-sided one- and two-storey wards and barracks and operating theatres turned into dorms and classrooms, connected by a network of covered ramps, corridors and tunnels. The curriculum was standard stuff, the teachers talented, committed people who worked very hard for low pay because of their religious commitment. They were more liberal than either the administration or the student body, and on the whole I flourished there.

The president of this somewhat strange operation was one J. Robert Ashcroft. Former evangelist, influential denominational fixer and insider, he will be remembered as the father of John Ashcroft, attorney general of the United States in George W. Bush's first administration. John's *Lessons From a Father to His Son* tells the story, widely circulated, that the elder Ashcroft, dying, anointed his son with ordinary cooking oil on the son's swearing-in as United States senator.

Over the next two years, during which I earned a BA in History, I came to Ashcroft's attention, as I would have in any case, with my beard and long hair and recycled Army kit, and bicycling everywhere with two little boys behind in a trailer, but chiefly because of the noisy part I played on behalf of Lyndon Johnson during the election of 1964 (the students were all for Barry Goldwater), and the barrage of samizdat I put out in response to Ashcroft's weirder chapel pronouncements, notably the prayer of thanksgiving one morning for the Good Friday earthquake of 1964 in Alaska. It seems the earthquake had made the fortune of an earth-moving contractor who had pledged money to the college building fund, but who had been close to bankruptcy and so would not have been able to fulfil his pledge except for a timely Act of God

Of the two times I sat in Ashcroft's office, one was to complain that I had been ignored in the annual announcements of academic distinction, even though I had the highest grade average in the college that year. Another time I had to seek his endorsement for a part-time job I wanted with a local radio station. On both occasions he explained, in a way that was at once so reasonable and so self-assured one felt obscurely ashamed to have taken up his time, that I did not properly represent the spirit of the college or of the denomination, or, for all I knew, of Missouri as well. Which was, I had to admit, true.

Ashcroft himself was both remote and unctuous, and in appearance an oddly artifical or mechanical character. He wore suits the way Richard Nixon did, as a sort of squarish padded armour that only hinted at a body underneath. The face was puffy and pallid with a fixed false-teeth smile behind thin lips and a jaw that moved up and down as though on strings. Looking at him up close made you think irresistably of a big-nose joke-mask with horn-rimmed glasses attached. In the college yearbook, which I saved, he looks this way yet.

The thing that stood out in his office was a giant nameplate affair of wood and brass, triangular in cross-section, which, instead of having his title and a name, said RÉFLÉCHISSEZ—a most curious object which I like to think has since occupied the desk of an attorney general of the United States. I am reminded of it whenever I think of the little narrative that follows, the key scene of which takes places in this very office—although I was not, myself, present on that occasion. Alison told me about it.

The last summer I was at the college I needed an additional course in French. No regular course being offered that term, Alison agreed to tutor me. We met several times a week, at which sessions we did a bit of grammar or dictation, and then settled down to talking. We became good friends. Gradually

I learned a lot of her history, and she of mine. It was during this summer I had at least one of my run-ins with Ashcroft, and Alison was aware of a certain disapproval, filtering down through the college administration, that she was helping me that summer. But since she was not being paid to do it, there was little anyone could do. I thought they would simply be happy to be rid of me. Alison and I laughed a good deal about this. I thoroughly enjoyed our meetings that summer, and I think she did too. Sadly, we underestimated the malice in store.

Alison was one of those extremely fair people, white skin and white hair, sensitive pale eyes always blinking or hidden behind dark glasses, whose feelings and intentions are as a consequence not easily read. She was also unusually tall, and round-shouldered, and walked in a headlong stoop, unheeding, usually clutching books or papers to her chest. It did not take long to discover, however, that behind this awkward exterior was a proud intelligence and a romantic nature. Alison was something of an artistocrat. Old Connecticut money, horses and private schools, Wellesley, class of '43. Except for the war, there would have been the obligatory tour of Europe. It was a mystery to me that she was at the college at all, or in Missouri for that matter.

An even greater mystery lay in the fact that Alison was married to the college janitor. An illiterate, a dreamy and ineffectual man, courteous and inoffensive, dressed habitually in bib overalls and clodhoppers, shorter than Alison, but lean and darkly handsome, he was often to be seen leaning on his broom in out of the way corners of the campus, or carrying plumbing implements somewhere in no great hurry. They had a daughter, an unconventional beauty, a student at the college, who was often seen with either of her parents, but not, to my recollection, with both of them together.

The mystery was in part unravelled in the course of the summer. In her characteristically indirect and ironical way, in little dropped fragments, between lip-pursing gouts of Wellesley-flavoured French, Alison told me that on graduation in 1943, Europe being closed because of the war, she went on a mission to Appalachia, under the auspices of some well-intentioned electrification-and-literacy scheme, and found herself instead overwhelmed by a culture more vital and earthy than anything she had ever before encountered or imagined. She was converted in a little mountain Pentecostal church and fell in love with a mountain man and eventually bore his child and was disowned by her family and all her former connections. She had never looked back.

Still this did not explain how they came to be at the college, and I did not discover the truth until the very last week of the summer term, at our final meeting together.

Alison arrived late, apologized, tried to begin our French review, but quickly broke down into sobbing. I confess I was at a loss for what to do about the naked distress of this woman, whom I liked, but who was older than me and physically awkward. I must have managed to bleat something encouraging. She blew her nose, dabbed at her eyes, and told me what happened.

She was late for our meeting because she had been called to Ashcroft's office, she said. Ashcroft told her he was letting her husband go. Telling her before telling him—itself a calculated insult—and said that he was forced to do it because her husband was not up to the work, and was anyway an embarrassment to the school, however entertaining and picturesque a fixture. He was not able to read manuals and written instructions or to complete reports and inventories. What was wanted was to put the housekeeping on a more regular and professional footing. The college was moving ahead aggressively with accreditation and a building programme (thanks to the Good Friday Alaska earthquake), and many regrettable decisions had to be made in the interest of the general good of the college, and so forth.

To make her humiliation complete, Alison said, she had to remind Ashcroft that she had come to the college—this was the first I heard this from her—on the condition that her husband was hired as well. In return for this she had accepted a salary reduced by so much as her husband was paid. The delicate and unspoken, but clearly understood, contract was that the college got a qualified and devoted French teacher on the cheap, and her husband was afforded a means of preserving his dignity as an earner of bread. Was Ashcroft prepared to keep her husband on in some capacity, Alison asked, if she voluntarily took a further cut in pay? If he was not prepared to do this she would have to leave the college, although it would not be easy for her to find another situation. She was not prepared, she told him, to see her husband disgraced in front of his daughter.

Having manoeuvred things to just the place he had sought all along, Ashcroft said smoothly that she, Alison, had put her finger on the problem exactly, and had also suggested the solution. A shakeup of the faculty was coming, he confided. A forward-looking college needed to increase the number of lecturers with PhDs. This misunderstanding about the terms of her contract was perhaps providential, as facing reality now would spare her an inevitable dismissal down the road. In consideration of her quite understandable concern for the feelings of her husband and daughter, and although this was an irregularity in his duty to the position he held, he would not dismiss her husband, if she, Alison, would tender her own resignation effective immediately. He would be pleased, it should go without saying, to write a most positive letter of recommendation, noting her many years of loyal service. He pulled out a letter of resignation he had prepared for her and she signed it.

I saw Alison a few years later, at the state university where I went to do graduate work. She had completed an MA, had found a job at a college in the upper Middle West somewhere, and was in town attending a workshop for French teachers. I asked after her husband and her daughter. She said they were fine.

The Artist of the Prayer Room

We were all late children, our parents older Norwegians of austere pietist views. Some of us had older siblings. These older siblings married one another and adopted the culture of the parents. But their adolescence was from before the war. We, on the other hand, grew up in the late forties and early fifties, and experimented with lipstick and cigarettes. For amusement, we rode the subway, to Coney Island, and to "the city," which meant Central Park, The Museum of Natural History, Hayden Planetarium, Greenwich Village, sometimes The Cloisters, the Frick. We also rode the Staten Island ferry.

There were crushes, and much speculative intrigue of a romantic nature, but we had no money and were not welcome in one another's houses. Outer clothing in those days was stiff and heavy and smelled in winter, and female underwear still a forbidden zone of crinolines and vests and garter clips, so we engaged mainly in kissing, a clumsy and unpleasant affair of chapped lips and dried spit on cold faces. This was anyway an exclusively winter sport, connected with Sunday afternoons after Sunday school and church. In the summer, Sunday school disbanded, church attendance fell off, and the gang dispersed to camp, to family cottages, to relatives in the country, to summer jobs, or, for those of us whose parents had neither cars nor cottages, to the damp chlorinated squalor of the swimming pool. What we lacked in sexual experience we made up for in psychological games of exquisite complexity and cruelty.

Eventually the gang broke up. Some families moved to Long Island. People left the church to join other sects, or, what was worse, formed splinters of their own. When this happened, which was frequent in the 40s and 50s, we could not henceforth speak to those people or to their children. We divided up along lines of money and culture and aspirations and of course of sex; the easy camaraderie of the subway rides to zoos and museums and the innocent and promiscuous kissing on front steps ended, and gave way to best friends and serious romances and the pull of the different high schools and colleges we went to. We did not, as older brothers and sisters had done, marry the people we grew up with. It was many years until I had a chance to meet anyone again from those days.

I had flown to LaGuardia from Toronto and hired a car and,

having appointments in Cape Cod and in New York, had decided to cross the Sound from Port Jefferson, drive to the Cape, and coming back take the ferry from New London to Orient Point, and so on to the city. This meant traversing the length of Long Island on an early Sunday morning, with little traffic and only the evocative place names for company: Smithtown, Babylon, Ronkonkoma, Valley Stream. Places of summer jobs, ancient picnics, places people had disappeared to. I decided at the last minute to drop in on the Brooklyn church, see if it was still there, attend a service perhaps.

The corner building on Fourth Avenue looked much as it had always done, a former Jewish Temple in the favoured classical style with pillars, broad steps and iron palings. It was now called a community church, a youthful congregation with a multicultural cast, but still with a Norwegian pastor to whom the old affiliations remained important. I might not have stayed for the morning service—the special entertainment being Mr. Gospel Trumpeteer, an evangelist based in Florida but descended from one of the old families—except that Leo was there too, my best friend from when we were ten and eleven.

Leo and I were now both in mid-career, he was in publishing, I was a university lecturer, we were both divorced and remarried, both with grown children. The meeting was a disaster from the beginning.

I was astonished to learn that he remembered me chiefly with resentment. I reminded him of an old photo of the two of us, ten-year-olds, arms across one another's shoulders, something I had treasured. He recalled the image and, with rancour, that I had been the taller of the two of us.

I took him and his new wife to dinner at the last Norwegian restaurant in Brooklyn. The new wife disliked the food, Leo resented that I had spoken to his mother before she died, and resented that as a consequence I had important things to tell him about his parents and about his mother's last days.

He thought I had been a threat to him when we were children. We had been rivals, it turned out. Rivals above all, he said, to my surprise, for the attentions of our friend Nikki. Nikki and I, he intimated, were the only ones he thought of as worthy opponents, the "intellectuals," as he put it—absurdly—in our crowd. Then he insinuated that there had been something more than kissing between him and Nikki, maybe some degree of petting beyond what was usual in the subways and on the front steps in winter, maybe even something more than that.

This clumsy attempt to gain an advantage nevertheless brought back in the following weeks a flood of memories, and a growing speculative interest in Nikki. I would say Nikki and me, if one could even speak thus of something so devoid of narrative or even episode. In those days she was still called

Anniken. I sometimes walked her home and we sat and talked on her stoop until her father rapped on the window.

I recalled that Nikki had been a beauty, a wide downturned mouth like a Swedish actress, lively quizzical eyes. Nikki was willful and imaginative. She had teased me more than once, from the time we were children, that we would live together when we were old in the *gamlehjem*, the Norwegian old-people's home, where church picnics were sometimes held because of the extensive grounds, and where we were startled as children by the wrinkled faces and vacant stares and the starched mob-caps of old women sitting in the windows.

Then another distinct memory, from later.

We must have been seventeen or eighteen; the last time I saw her until much, much later, after my visit with Leo. I had walked her home from some event at church, as we had used to do, and we sat for many hours on the stone steps next to an area with a rose-of-Sharon bush enclosed in iron palings. We talked about our experiences and plans. I remember a rigmarole of a story about a man from work—an office in the city somewhere—who had taken her to a rooftop party. She drank too much. She remembered staying on. Someone fondling her breasts or stroking her belly. And being undressed. I did not know what the point of her saying all this was supposed to be. Flaunting? Teasing? Mocking? A proposal? I only know that I felt a peculiar desolation. A conviction that I was out of my depth. Anger at my own lack of experience.

As I said, I did not see Nikki again until much later, the summer after I saw Leo.

Nikki now lived in a small city in south-central Pennsylvania. Not so very far from Brooklyn, where again I had some business. Verrazano and Goethals bridges, the New Jersey Turnpike, the Pennsylvania Turnpike to the Reading exit. Four hours on a pleasantly hot summer afternoon with the air-conditioning on and the radio full of Oliver North and Admiral Poindexter; it was the summer of Iran-Contra.

I called Nikki from the Treadway Inn outside of town. I said I was passing through and had a free evening. A breezy intelligent voice with traces of a Brooklyn accent said she was going out to dinner with a friend, but come over, we could all go out together. I demurred. She said well it is a woman friend so it's no bother. She said her daughter would come over and show me the way.

I asked what the daughter looked like.

Some jokey asides with another female voice in the background.

"She's driving a blue Toyota. She says she looks like a scumbag."

Nikki was well off. Divorced from a successful lawyer. A son, who was not at home, was something in films. The beautiful daughter, who liked dropping words like "scumbag," pursued a course at a local college. When Nikki came down to meet me she was wearing a too-youthful taffeta skirt. Probably borrowed from the daughter, I thought ungenerously. I said she hadn't changed a bit, which was partly true. The same ashy-blonde hair, now more art than nature, the same down-turned mouth. In the old snapshots Nikki had always worn a scowl. She had two strong lines that ran downward from the corners of her mouth. A determined face. Laughing eyes, blue-grey, a certain tautness over the cheekbones, a slightly jutting jaw, a faraway look in unguarded moments, a very Norwegian face.

The town-house she lived in was a smart horror of flounces and bad pictures. She showed me around her town. We talked about the past. She had a great fund of stories from the old days, stories from the hidden world of women. Of two sisters seduced by their step-father, a pillar of the church, an elder and former missionary to India. The mother of one of our gang who flushed a foetus down the toilet to protect an older sister. The couple who had sex regularly during church services, slipping out and dashing off to his family's house in his MG sports-car. Nikki tried to project a coarse relish in this tittle-tattle.

She also kept dropping hints about a young boyfriend—his youthfulness was insisted upon—a carpenter, with a pickup truck and a toolbox. She mentioned the toolbox twice. I felt an old desolation beginning to creep over me.

I went back to the Treadway Inn to shower and change. Nikki picked me up later, and we went to get her friend. The friend's name was Rhoda and she lived next door to the house where Nikki had lived with her husband. Rhoda was also an abandoned wife, although still in possession of her suburban acres. Seeing her old house was clearly upsetting for Nikki. It was an ugly brick thing, and Nikki had in her time put on an addition with appalling faithfulness to the dull original and its graceless windows. Now someone was making it over again, with the addition of screening-walls with port-hole openings. "Post-modern," Nikki said disapprovingly. Nikki regretted the grand fund-raising lawn parties she used to throw, and all the friends she used to have. She told me how she had been cheated out of this house by her husband. Nikki had stuck with him through years of infidelity (his), and neglect and helplessness (hers). When it came time to turn this around, he got expensive psychotherapy and she got drugs. In the middle of this therapeutic regime he left her anyway, landing her in an asylum to dry out, with her kids at home with no food.

We had a pleasant dinner. Rhoda was taking a course at the local college. We talked about that, and about Ollie North. Nikki and I tried to explain to her about growing up in a Pentecostal church, and about speaking in tongues, and about being Norwegian. Some of this was very funny. After we dropped Rhoda off, we went to Nikki's house and talked until late.

Nikki remembered her childhood as a happy one. Her parents were in love, and there were many intimations of a robust sex life between them. Her father had been a master machinist. He made lamps out of artillery shells, she said, although Nikki does not own one. A wealthy aunt kept Nikki and her sister supplied with expensive dresses and expensive summer holidays. Nikki remembered this still with a keen and childlike pleasure.

Her sister, Nikki said, does not remember her childhood in quite this same light. She seemed mainly to remember her father as the ogre people commonly remember strict parents to be. Nikki saw an irony in this, as the sister is still a born-again Christian and Nikki is not.

Nikki remembers her father through the filter of her experience of marriage. Her father, in her view, for all his strictness was adequate in a way her husband wasn't. Her father gave his wife his full affection, indulgently, without reserve. She thought that was what a real man did. Although Nikki thought that her childhood was, on the whole, a happy one, she was resentful about the church, and told me an interesting story.

Her father believed that while it was true as a general principle that one mustn't lie, one might tell a lie under certain circumstances—to protect a friend, for example, or to earn a livelihood. In this spirit, Nikki had not only found herself a job for which she had to lie about her age, but had agreed with her boss, in order to cover the inconvenient fact that she looked too young, to wear lipstick at work, although this was strictly forbidden by the rule of the church. Lipstick was equivalent to smoking or going to the movies.

As chance would have it, she was spotted wearing lipstick downtown by an elder of the church, a thick-headed reformed drunk whose own daughters flouted freely the spirit of the dress codes. If lipstick was taboo, they used heavy face powders. They wore no earrings, which were forbidden, but bought flashy necklaces, bracelets—even anklets. If dresses must have demure sleeves that covered the shoulders, their hemlines crept provocatively above the knee.

This pillar of respectability duly reported to the members-only business-and-communion meeting held monthly in the church basement that Nikki was seen wearing lipstick in public. I don't recall what she told me was the immediate consequence of this. No doubt a solemn warning about her witness before the world, and the perils of vanity, and the danger of backsliding.

Some while after this—a year or more, she said—Nikki was at a party for another girl in the church, a wedding shower, with a tissue-paper throne for the honoured guest and small gifts of housewares and the like on display, and pot-luck refreshments. At the end, as people were leaving, someone reported five dollars missing from a purse. When this came to the attention of the elders, it was remembered that Nikki, of those present, had most recently come to their attention for discipline. Clearly, a person who would wear lipstick would steal. Nikki was given the lie direct. She must have taken the five dollars. The pastor himself convened a sort of kangaroo court and tried to bluster her into a confession. They failed to break her. Nikki remembers that her mother stood by her, and told the elders in a trembling voice that her Anniken was a good girl, and would not steal five dollars or tell lies.

Nikki was amusing on the old women in our milieu, whose lives were spent hugging and rocking themselves in self-pity and regret, with those peculiar, sharp, in-taken Norwegian sighs, lines of weariness and quiet despair permanently stamped on their faces. Nikki was very good at imitating these gestures and intonations. More than any of us in our circle, Nikki and her sister had grown up with Norwegian as the primary household language, and she had a genius for accents, but with a touch of hysteria that went beyond parody. The image of the rocking and self-hugging old ladies was clearly a terror for her, the nightmare she lived with. All this cast an interesting, and poignant, light, I thought, on Nikki's suburban appearance and demeanour, the brittle American middle-age she had chosen.

It also brought to mind again the odd idea she had when we were children, the one that we would meet in the *gamlehjem* when we were old. A detail of this fantasy came to me: she used to say that we would dig a tunnel between the old ladies' part and the old men's part, and sneak visits to one another.

We had arranged I would come back the next morning for coffee before saying goodbye. After the intensity of the night before I felt drained, and disappointed in myself. Nikki and I were the same age, but I felt I had been too old, too dull, that I had failed to rise to something that must still be there, was always there, and was now receding for good because I could not think what to say or do and lacked the essential courage to seize whatever it might be. I felt both relief and regret that this was over, I could not even imagine what I might have wanted, what I might have desired out of it all. Self-absorbed in this way I had not given much thought to what Nikki might have thought of the evening and of what had been said, nor thought really much about her life, as something someone had lived and was living. I realized with sadness that her life was unimaginable to me except as certain stories and recollected emotions from long ago. We were strangers to one another.

I was expecting Nikki to appear that morning the smart suburban matron she had first wanted me to see, and was surprised when I arrived to find that she looked as though she had not slept very well. She was serious and pensive. She stood directly in the harsh light of a window without any make-up and looked straight at me with the utmost frankness.

"Hello," I said.

"Do you want to see the rest of the house?" she said, "I haven't shown you upstairs."

"Maybe we can do that, " I said.

The coffee had been made and she poured some into mugs and we sat down in her sitting room on opposite sides of a huge coffee table of limed ash. She made no move to show me the upstairs. We sat in silence for a while.

Then she said, without preamble, "I am an abandoned woman."

She had spoken, the night before, about her marriage, the failures and injustices. But there was now something new in her tone. The practiced ironies of the divorcée, the stagey brittle cynicism, were gone. She was appealing for something. Not justice. Or consolation. Maybe understanding.

"But you are free now," I said. "You survived. You have a home, successful children."

"I was a virgin when I married," she said. "I bought a nightie to wear for my husband on our wedding night and he said that it showed I had a dirty mind. He found me disgusting. After the children came he said he was impotent and that it was my fault. But I discovered he made love to other women. He must have found me so disgusting he had rather be thought impotent than make love to me.

"I am still the prisoner of my vows. I have not had sex in twenty years."

She had not shed a tear or raised her voice.

There had been no rooftop sex, no carpenter lover. Leo's insinuations had been lies.

Nikki was magnificent in her ruin, her anger, her pride, her stubbornness, the extravagant waste of it all.

I finished my coffee and we said goodbye. I've not seen her since. The sharpest memory I retain of Nikki, however, is not this goodbye, but something from much earlier.

The former Reform Temple used by the church for meetings still had, in my childhood, its ornate wooden ark at the front, now adapted to house the baptismal tank. JESUS in gilt gothic letters had been added to its pediment. Nothing else had been changed, but in the basement, in a bit of left-over space between the boiler room and the kitchen, the elders had constructed what came to be called simply the prayer room, a charmless, windowless, carpeted room with no furnishings or decoration, only a built-in kneeling bench running all around the irregular shape of the room.

This unprepossessing place was the nerve centre or power source for the spiritual project of the Pentecostal congregation. It was where pastors and evangelists went for inspiration, kneeling before an open Bible in prayerful attitude. Where whole nations of the heathen were converted by the heroic intercessions of a handful of elderly female prayer-warriors. Where the young people repaired after Sunday evening services in order to achieve, under the gaze of watchful brothers and sisters, the Baptism in the Holy Ghost, the crowning initiation into adulthood and full membership in our sect, and which when properly achieved was marked by gusts of ecstatic gibberish from a prostrate and exhausted seeker.

The solemnity of these occasions was not in any way diminished by the circumstance that through the walls on Sunday evenings, from the community centre next door, which the Jewish congregation had retained when they sold the Temple, could be heard the muted noise of laughter, and dancing, and the minor-key orientalism of a klezmer band.

Nikki was without doubt the artist of the prayer room. Ever seeking, never consoled. No one wept with more abandon. No one tarried longer. An image comes to mind, whether of one occasion or many I cannot say: Nikki's face red and swollen from prolonged weeping; sprawled, her head on one arm on the kneeling bench, the rest of her half-reclined, one leg tucked up under her skirt, the other extended on the carpeted floor, a flat shoe whitened with chalky polish in the manner of those days, a still-shapeless schoolgirl calf exposed below the hem of a navy-blue dress.

Pont Neuf

There aren't many good Ayatollah Khomeini stories, and who cares any more. Soon no one will know who you mean, although he was no joke, with those murderous eyes and his tremendous sadness. I know a story in which he figured in a small way, and I know it is true because I got it from a friend.

We had drifted out of touch. I knew Dave's marriage of many years had broken up, but little else. We had in fact seen one another relatively seldom, even during the years that we were close, but in the way of some friendships, maybe the best ones, it didn't seem to matter. We would write or ring now and then, and meet when we could. On occasion we would contrive to get invited to the same conferences, preferably in exotic places, and without ever saying so explicitly, arranged that our wives would not find it agreeable or convenient to come along, it being a rule of our friendship to keep our families out of it, or at least out of its serious recesses, and only to talk of wives, or women for that matter, in the most carefully and ambiguously ironic way.

Our friendship was based on irony, as though to admit anything deeply felt, would be to admit a degree of intimacy that might put the friendship at risk, unbalance it in ways that might have been impossible to rectify. Besides, I think we both enjoyed our mildly anarchic holidays from seriousness.

We had cultivated a sort of sideline, in our professional and literary pursuits, in which we posed as fellow-travellers, or as donnish "students," of one hare-brained scheme or outlandish theory or another, usually religious—chairing meetings, giving papers at obscure conferences, sometimes even posing "solutions" to their mind-numbing conundrums, only to relish seeing our own minted rubbish return again and again in earnest guise. We became, through these intermittent exercises, connoisseurs of the ridiculous.

It was at one of these meetings that I heard the Khomeini story from Dave, a recounting which, I can see in retrospect, was the beginning of the end of our friendship, although that had nothing to do with the confessional content of his story, which, as you will see, was minimal. The decline of our friendship may have had more to do with the inevitable collapse of anything based so exclusively on irony.

We were in the Caribbean, in 1989 I think, at a new resort on the French half of an island the other side of which was Dutch and which was in possession of the only airport. To get to this resort you had to hire a car and drive for several hours over terrible roads, past black peasant settlements of chickens, scrawny men, big women in bright plastic hair rollers, beaten earth under trees that looked like giant broccoli, then over some jagged mountains, to a secluded green crescent on the sea that was a filled-in marsh, with a beach that had been trucked in, and a lavish white, arcaded hotel in three sections formed around a pool and a bar.

The meeting was to be a "dialogue" between Jesuits and an oriental sect that drew on both Christian and Buddhist ideas, the whole being paid for by a Jewish intellectual in Washington who ran a right-wing think-tank that mostly pandered to Latin American generals and police chiefs, and who had been put up to this by Dave, who had advanced to the stage of thinking up these capers instead of waiting for them to happen.

Dave was already depressed about the meeting. The only Jesuit he could get was an elderly whisky-priest in exile in Paraguay for some ancient misdemeanor, and who arrived drunk, having been routed by way of Los Angeles. There was, in compensation, a terribly intelligent and sincere American nun with a blue cloth pinned on the back of her head who read papers no one understood, and a British woman, horsy, with big teeth and big yellow hair and trousers that were too short, who was supposed to have been an academic, but turned out to be some sort of journalist who snapped pictures everywhere with a Rollei, and gushed over the most stupefying inanities. For the rest there were only po-faced Asians and an assortment of free-loaders, including a Norwegian theologian who went everywhere with white cream on his nose and in his arm-pits. Not that any of this mattered; it suited our sponsors merely to be able to report that this "dialogue" had taken place, but I could see it was making Dave pensive and that the fun had gone temporarily out of our traffic in absurdities.

On the second day of this meeting, Dave and I were sitting near the pool, under an umbrella, drinking coffee. It was early enough in the morning for a touch of freshness in the air. There were no other guests in the resort hotel, for this was off-season for the well-heeled European tourists the place was designed for, and the management were training a new intake of young employees, brought over from France, who seemed to do little but make lying about seem a particularly refined art form.

From where we were sitting that morning we could see a slender young man in a horizontally striped cotton jersey and loose navy trousers standing, quite still, looking at the sea. Nearer to hand, at the bar, a young girl perched on a stool with nothing on except a white singlet and washed-out skimpy mauve knickers, and studied her painted toe-nails. By the pool a man with a large professional-looking camera and his female assistant were trying to get a promotional photo shot, in which a naked girl is caught in the act of leaping up out of the water in the pool with droplets of water flying everywhere. The object was to get her at the height of her leap, with her expression just so, and the water just so, and, from the nature of much explicit but good-natured gesturing, it was clear, also, to have her breasts, which were round and heavy, just at the right elevation, and not looking painfully up in the air, or sagging, and so she could not be snapped at the very top of her leap but just near it, and this more than anything took many, many attempts: The camera would be positioned, the girl would disappear under the water, then she would explode into view, arms wide to make the most splash, and then she would fall back again. Each time, there would be a shrug from the man with the camera, a discussion with many languid gestures, the girl would climb out of the pool and pull a towel around her, and there would be a long wait in which they were very still, and said nothing, and smoked a cigarette, and then they would start again.

During one of these breaks, Dave said, without actually looking at me, "I never told you my Ayatollah Khomeini story." I looked over at him to see if this were a joke. I was sure I had heard him correctly. Something about his look made me keep silent, and I waited for the story.

"This was in 1978. I was in England with Barbara, in Oxford, and things were not going well." Dave paused.

This was new territory for us, and I waited, keeping my eyes mostly on the photographer and the naked girl while he talked.

"I made a trip to Paris that fall. Flew over for a weekend. The first trip I ever made to France. Although I saw it once."

I looked over at him. Dave smiled.

"France," he explained, "In the army in Germany, I had to drive somebody to a place near Strasbourg, and saw France in the distance.

"Anyway, I had a pretext for this jaunt to Paris, something I was going to see in a museum. I didn't really need to. I wanted to get away for a little while. As I said, Barbara and I weren't getting along. I went up to London the night before and stayed overnight with a young couple we knew from Canada who had a room in Finchley Road. They put me up on the floor and I slipped out in the morning before they were up and got the tube to the airline office where you could catch a bus to Heathrow. It was still dark out and the streets were wet from rain. There was hardly anyone on the bus; only me, and a woman.

"She sat ahead of me two or three seats and across the aisle. All I remember taking in at this point is that she was perhaps Indian or Arab, and rich. You could tell from the shoes, the bag, the coat, very conservative, very expensive, even the head scarf.

"It occurred to me that it was odd, this woman being on a

bus at this hour of the morning going to the airport. I mean, wouldn't she have a limo or something? Or her husband's Mercedes? It didn't make sense. Also she didn't have any luggage except her bag, and a matching carrier that wasn't much bigger, and she was fumbling with a ticket and maps that she kept opening and closing as though these were things she had no experience of and wasn't sure what to do with.

"About half way to the airport, this woman suddenly turned and looked at me. I mean she turned all the way around and looked me full in the face. 'Are you going to Paris, too?' she said, as though Paris was the last stop for this bus we were on, as though we weren't going to a major airport where people could be going anywhere in the world.

"'Yes, I am,' I said.

"'Good,' she said, and turned around again, as though something were settled, and stopped fiddling with her ticket and maps.

"As soon as the bus stopped, she went forward and down the steps, and was waiting for me when I got out. Without any preliminary, as though this followed from my saying Yes and her saying Good, she held her ticket out for me to inspect. 'You will hold this for me, please, and let me come along with you. I do not know where to go, and I do not understand what it says on there.' There was maturity and strength in the voice and in the gaze, but also the most amazing child-like innocence. I say that, but she was not really like a child. It wasn't innocence really. It was rather as though an immense experience of the world had made her trust me in this moment because that was the safest thing to do, and nothing in her experience had left room for being conventionally coy. I could not imagine the up-bringing or the manner of life that would have produced this woman. It unsettled me, to say the least. I even felt a bit afraid, in a cowardly physical way. This woman must belong to somebody. I was going to become embroiled in a nasty incident with brothers-in-law in leather coats and little moustaches, men with implacable eyes, who would cut off a joint of my little finger, and this woman would accept this as normal behaviour and get in their Mercedes and be speeded away, maybe only looking back once, her face visible in a single flash of illumination from the mercury-vapour lamp over the road, sad-eyed and pale, with purple lips, through the rear window."

Dave was clearly in better spirits. His voice had risen in parodistic hysteria at this movies image. We both laughed.

I went and disturbed mauve knickers for more coffees, and when they were ready brought them back. The slender man in the blouse had disappeared. The sun had moved higher and the photographer and his assistant had decided to quit for the time and went inside. The naked girl was absorbed in rubbing oil on her body for an afternoon's sun-bathing. Black-skinned housemaids in white uniforms glided silently from time to time on obscure errands behind the shaded arcades of the hotel building opposite us. I adjusted the umbrella, to keep us in the shade.

"But chivalry prevailed?" I prompted him.

"Well, what was I to do?" Dave said. " For a single mad moment I thought she was going to take my hand, or my arm. It was like we were married. We didn't talk. We walked together to the terminal and went through all the rigmarole one has to go through, and got seats together on this flight to Paris. And I was enjoying it. Being catapulted into another life, with another woman. No stages in between. No getting to know someone. It was more intimate than you can imagine. More than I imagine an affair must be."

I looked sharply at him when he said this, wondering if he realized what he had just revealed about himself.

But Dave continued without a pause. "When we were seated on the plane, she said, 'You must know Paris very well.' I made a gesture that I hoped looked like modesty.

"'Perhaps you could tell me how to get to,' and she hesitated over the strange word, 'Pont Neuf.'

"There was never any small talk between us, about the weather, or where we lived, or what we did. I don't think she ever asked for my name. There were only these very direct and trusting requests.

"I said I wasn't sure where it was but that it was a bridge and that I had a guide book and I would look it up. I had one of those little blue hard-cover travel guides that I had picked up at a second-hand stall, filled with complicated walking tours and engraved maps, quarter by quarter, with every alley and lane marked out, and obscure literary and historical associations noted for each. Absolutely hopeless for anything a modern tourist needs, really, but it did have bridges, and I opened out the tipped-in large-scale map, on fragile india paper and no bigger than a handkerchief, and put my finger on the Pont Neuf as we put our heads together over this absurd little book.

"She turned on me a look of purest delight, as one will with a particularly clever child, and looked down again at the ridiculous map and at my finger on the Pont Neuf, as though at a treasure map whose riddle has been solved, as though I were in possession of the one document in the world that would guide her to her destination—about which she apparently knew nothing.

"Also, she apparently knew nothing of where we would land, how we would get into the city, and how one might get around in the city. Nor did I, really. I like to arrive in strange places with nothing more useful than a guide of the type I had, get into the middle of things by following the crowd, and look around. It works if you leave plenty of time, and I had the entire day ahead of me, with no particular plans. I told her this, which she took to be the most clever sort of plan, genius really, and could she follow me into the city, and when we were close to the Pont Neuf, I would point her to it. Then she said she had to be there exactly at noon.

"In all this while I never got to have a really good look at her face. We were one way and another always beside each other. When we stood she stood very close, and when we sat on the plane together she leaned slightly on the arm of the seat toward me and her head was always slightly inclined towards me. She was not a very young woman. More than that I could not say. I had no impression of her body, although she was slim. She had long, narrow feet, in impractical black patent shoes with fairly high heels, and thin, straight calves. She never removed her coat, which was a slate-grey mackintosh, although I seem to remember a high-necked soft blouse visible at the top. Her features were, I suppose, regular, and her skin colour was quite dark. Her hands were not pretty. They were slightly misshapen, with large purplish knuckles.

"What I chiefly remember was her smell, the smell of old wood and bitter oranges, and something sour-salty, like the smell of a crying child's breath. Her hair, when she removed her head scarf, was thick and clean and glistened with little lights. It fell in waves. slightly tangled, nearly to her shoulder. I sat during the silences with my eyes closed, intensely conscious of her hair inches away.

"Perhaps the spell I was under will explain why I had not asked her the reason she had to be on the Pont Neuf at noon.

She nevertheless, after a long interval, in her own strangely direct and naive way, told me why she had come to Paris.

"'Do you have a hotel?' she began.

"'No,' I said.

"She opened her bag and pulled out a piece of paper and handed it to me. 'That is the hotel I am in.' The paper was a teletype confirmation and said that a room was reserved for a Mme Moussani for one night's lodging with breakfast at the Hotel Washington-Opéra. The date was that day.

"'You must go to this hotel and get a room for tonight,' she said, with the air of one pleased that she too is capable of solving problems. 'I hear it is very good. And then I will see you there later.'

"I cannot tell you the state this put me in. There was not the slightest suggestion of anything sexual in her proposition. It was on the face of it, a straight quid pro quo: I would get her to the Pont Neuf, she would direct me to a hotel. Yet it was the very simplicity of it, indeed its naturalness, that opened an abyss of moral dilemma. The thing was, this invitation was *tempting*, which is always a sign. I should have made some excuse. Thanked her. Let it go."

When Dave got to this point in his narrative I remembered that he was a Catholic, which I had forgotten. In the back of my mind I was thinking of some way to interject some levity, tease him a bit. But Dave was in full flood and I could see no way to interrupt.

"I desired her, you see, more than I could have thought possible. I imagined entering a hotel room and removing her clothes and seeing her hair spread on a pillow and her narrow body outlined on a sheet. I could see her arms and her knees and the circles of her sunken aureoles like pools of blood, and I would bend over her and smell the hair under her arms and on her mound and place my hand in the space between her thighs.

"All the while I was seized with the most craven fear and self-contempt. I could see myself with cruel accuracy: a tall, stooped Canadian inclined to sentimentality, affecting to look British in cavalry twills and a houndstooth jacket and a viyella shirt and brogues too big for my feet. I was tormented with the idea she would laugh at me, was perhaps laughing at me now.

"I wrote down the name of the hotel, and the phone number, and her name.

"'Mme Moussani,' I said experimentally, deliberately giving it a French inflection, scarcely able to breathe.

"'My husband,' she said, looking at me with a level gaze, and speaking softly, 'is in Teheran. He is in the Shah's government. There is an Iranian holy man you have perhaps read about in the papers. He is living in exile, surrounded by his followers, somewhere in Paris.' She made a small dismissive gesture with her hand. 'I know nothing about it. I have a message for him,' she said after a pause, and touched her bag. 'Someone will come from him to meet me on this Pont

Neuf and take me to him. I will give him the message, they will bring me back, and that is all I have to do.' She smiled brightly.

"This was before the revolution in Iran of course. I had read somewhere about Khomeini, although I could not have come up with the name, or his religious title, and I don't think she mentioned it at any time. In any case, I had too much to digest to make much of any of it, much less calculate any danger to her or to me in what she had said. The word husband registered, and Iranian, and behind the naivety, now definitely I thought I saw a protective mask lift slightly, a gentle sadness, perhaps even sorrow. I was entirely out of my depth, but I also now felt the calm one must feel who has accepted his fate.

"There was no more opportunity for talk. The plane landed at Charles de Gaulle. There was a long bus ride to the Porte Maillot in a heavy morning mist that made it impossible to see anything. The bus was full and we were forced to sit apart. Mme Moussani—I have no other name for her—kept looking at me as though for reassurance, although I could not imagine what she was really thinking.

"At the Porte Maillot we plunged immediately into the Métro and stopped in front of an illuminated map of the system. I got out my pathetic little guide book and roughly aligned the map with the one on the wall. I found a station close to the Pont Neuf that she could get to directly, and picked another for myself, somewhere along the Champs-

Elysées. I repeated the directions to her several times. She said she understood and would go there now, so she would be sure not to miss her rendezvous. I said as casually as I could that perhaps we would check with each other at the hotel, let's say at six, and perhaps think about getting something to eat. She treated this also as a brilliant plan that solved everything and she had no idea what she would have done with herself otherwise. And then she was gone.

"I emerged a little while later into brilliant sunshine from the Avenue Franklin D. Roosevelt station, which I had picked for no other reason than its sound, and realized with a shock that it was November 11th, Armistice Day, or whatever they call it now, and of course it was the sixtieth anniversary of the end of the First World War, and I was in Paris.

"A column of paratroopers in battle dress marched down the Champs-Elysées, followed by artillery pieces, and further along a gash of colour resolved into a troop of Zouaves. Bunting hung from every building, a military band played in the distance. From another direction came indistinct reverberations of an address over loudspeakers. Gents with ribbons on their overcoats, women with dark stockings with seams, young girls with tricolour ribbons in their hair, sullen blacks with pitted faces. Two men in short leather jackets and short hair suddenly grabbed an Arab-looking man in an identical leather jacket standing near the curb, and frog-marched him into a narrow alley-way between smart shops.

"I drifted along in what I took to be the direction of the hotel whose name I had on a piece of paper, not caring very much about the time, drinking in the smoky air and the light of a perfect autumn day.

"The hotel was surprisingly small, shabby even, in a little street near the Opéra-Comique. It had a modern plate-glass entrance and a tiny lift. The proprietor was a friendly man of some girth, who spoke a correct, rather American, English with outdated slang, picked up from GIs perhaps, and many Gallic shrugs. I paid for the cheapest room he had, which was a hundred francs, and went out again.

"Now everything turns comical and ridiculous. It was early afternoon and I had got hungry. But having paid for the room I realized that, foolishly, I had only taken about three hundred francs with me, over a hundred of which were now gone, and I had left behind my American Express card. I mentally set aside the francs I would need for the bus to the airport the next day, a few more for the Métro, and the remainder was appalling. I had told Mme Moussani we would go somewhere to eat. What a figure I would cut. I laughed bitterly out loud, and talked to myself, along the Seine, in and out of Notre-Dame, all over the Left Bank as far as Montparnasse and back again. On the quay along the Seine I allowed myself to be panhandled by a young couple who said they needed ten francs for the telephone and went away laughing. I cursed myself for a shmuck, wishing I were in different clothes. I wandered around the Opéra and sat in the church of the Madeleine for a while. Then it was nearly six o'clock.

"Well, as you will have guessed, she didn't show up at six o'clock. Or at seven. I asked the proprietor if Mme Moussani was registered. He said yes, her room was paid for and would be held all night. Each hour that passed I left a new message that I would be back within the hour. Each time I returned I got a sympathetic shrug. She never called to cancel the room or to leave any message.

"In between I walked up and down the boulevards, looking at people in the cafés, wolfish in mood by this time. I bought a bag of hot chestnuts from a charcoal brazier, which turned out to be the only food I ate that day, still hoarding my money although there was no longer any point in it. At midnight, after a final chat with the proprietor, who I think now looked on me with a certain pitying interest, I went up to my room. It was very small of course, with a sagging bed and a chipped armoire and dark purple wallpaper with flowers, but clean, the sheets stiff and sweet-smelling. The room faced on the street, directly above the entrance, and although it was on the fourth floor, I satisfied myself that with the window propped open slightly I could hear anyone being admitted below. I washed my face in the basin and lay down on the bed with all my clothes on, intending to listen in case Mme Moussani came in the night. But of course I was totally exhausted and fell into a deep sleep, from which I was only awakened by sun streaming through the window."

Here we were interrupted by a gaggle of conferees emerging from the hotel with plates of food. The lady journalist, whose name was Daisy, joined us, and then some others came over. I went in to get food, and Dave followed, picking over the vast buffet.

Outside, the sun was a laser, dispersing conversation and will into random meaningless twittery gestures. Light bounced from every conceivable surface, from the white hotel fronts, the sea, the plastic furniture. We all hid behind dark glasses. I pulled some copies of the day's seminar papers from under my chair, and settled into thinking about the work of the afternoon.

Dave was chairman of a long afternoon session. I watched him closely. He was entirely his most amusing self. He sat with his head in one hand, dreamily doodling on a yellow pad in front of him, while the reader of a paper droned on. Following the paper, he waited for the spate of technical objections and the bits of grand-standing to exhaust themselves, and then interjected, apologetically, as someone with no specialist knowledge of the Pali canon, or Bellarmine's defense of papal authority, some shrewd observation that placed the issue on an unexpected and higher plane of generality. Floating, as he always did, a phrase or a definition so apropos as to be repeated by others throughout the day in quite other contexts, slowly losing its attribution to him. At one point in the afternoon when this happened I caught his eye and got a barely perceptible wink. It was the old game, and I felt heartened.

Afterwards I didn't see him until dinner, which was laid out as a barbecue on the beach, a steel-drum band playing, and coloured lights strung up against the early tropical darkness. He was in animated conversation with a knot of the po-faced Asians. Their peculiar laughter, which sounded as though they were reading loudly together the words Ha Ha Ha but not quite in unison, carried clearly over the genial din of cracking lobster shells and the pingety-pong-pong-pingety of the steel-drum band and the contented chatter, and Dave looked happy, leaning forward, arms crossed, weight shifted first to one leg then the other.

It was very late, when the last remains of the party had left the beach, and some had gone off to bed, while others sat in little groups of three or four at the tables around the pool, that Dave and I found time to resume our conversation. We sat on deck chairs outside the ring of light from the pool and the bar, looking out to the sea, now inky and vast below a starlit sky.

I asked him if he had ever seen or heard from Mme Moussani again, after that night. He didn't answer immediately, and then sighed, and said no he hadn't, and had no idea what became of her.

"Did you think to make enquiries?" I asked, meaning to provoke.

"No, I don't suppose I did." He sounded a little surprised at the question, and impatient.

"You see," he continued, "when I woke in the morning, in that hotel, I realized I had escaped a terrible humiliation. I had most of a day in Paris ahead of me, absolutely nothing planned, and I was going to savour every minute of it. I washed up as best I could, put the slept-in clothes back on and went down to breakfast. Everything from then on went like a dream. The smallest things are engraved on my mind, as though the unreality of the day before had sharpened my senses. The croissants, and strong coffee in a bowl. The tiny tables set up in the reception area by the desk—the hotel had no dining room. Two women who had been in the hotel overnight chatting in German and giggling at something. A man who tried to pick them up and was rebuffed and returned to his newspaper. I wanted to laugh out loud for joy and relief.

"I laid out my francs, and set aside what I needed for the Métro and the bus, for the museum admission, for lunch and so forth, and put these amounts in different pockets. I took my guide book in hand and set out. It was Sunday, and the museum opened at ten and the admission was eight francs. When I got there—this was the decorative arts museum, I forget what they call it—I went straight to what I wanted to see, a medieval carving, a wooden saint. The figure was carved seated on a chair of a type that there are no actual surviving examples of. I was interested in those things in those days. I made some notes and dashed out again.

"I can't tell you what I didn't do. Walked everywhere. Ended up eating lunch in a horrible chromium and tinted-glass bar near the Luxembourg gardens. I can even tell you what I ate: a great fatty piece of lamb steak with smallish beans. It was wonderful.

"I decided to work my way back toward the Porte Maillot and catch the bus at about five o'clock. From Montparnasse, somewhere along the way, the train went above ground, and headed over the Seine near the Eiffel Tower, which I had never thought about, and would have despised going to see. But there it was, and I decided, on an impulse, to get off at the next station, which turned out to be Passy.

"I wandered there for a while on the steep little streets, and then to the Trocadero and sat on the steps among the families and the lovers, looking over at the Tower and the Invalides. On a corner of the Avenue Kléber I saw a pastry shop open. I counted all my francs again, and found I had sixty left beside the bus fare. In the window was something called a *tarte normande* for sixty francs. I can still see it, neat coils of apple slices, glazed and shining. I went in and pointed to it, and got it in a white pasteboard box with string around it, to take to Barbara.

"I walked toward the Arc and saw the sun shining low and golden in the limes down the length of Avenue Victor-Hugo.

Of course carrying this *tarte normande* carefully all the time. Sitting on the crowded bus with this thing on my lap, on the plane, through customs, on the train to Oxford. This little white box with a string around it. Barbara was tickled with it, of course. I got in very late. But we stayed up and ate it all."

We sat for a long while without saying anything. The stars, in a moonless sky, seemed to burn with increasing intensity. I thought to myself that I had no idea what direction we were facing, looking on the sea. Whether toward America, or Europe, or toward the North or South Pole.

Venus on the Malecón

"The African ass, *le cul africain,* lights everywhere in inexhaustible variety. Present even in indexical indirection, in the small excess of sacral tilt, the deeper tuck where bum meets thigh, the hint of a too-small waist, an unexpected cantilever, an incipient gluteal bloom, these are the delicious genetic markers that give away the history of a race. Then here and there its complete flowering: Great jodhpurs-haunches; high, deep, spherical buttocks. Like an old brandy-flask among bottles, this unruly exuberance achieves the final logic of the female body, the final setting out of sex as form. And when, among these rare blooms, as one may see on any evening in the promenade along the Malecón, such a specimen wears nothing more than a pair of plastic flip-flops and a harlequin body stocking, outsize black-and-white lozenges mapping as they celebrate her contours, leaving absolutely nothing uncharted and unrevealed to the gaze . . ."

I wrote those words in Cuba some years ago, in a bad imitation of Roland Barthes, in a spiral-bound notebook with lurid parrots on the cover.

There are other things in the notebook.

Notes, for example, on a paper to be called "Teaching Culture in a Time of Terror." This was long before the attacks of September 11, in the days when Carlos Fuentes mused in print on why an American President could not contrive to be alone with his woman long enough to have his trousers properly off. Thus I may be excused for having placed under the rubric of Terror the absence of the ironical and the metaphysical, the pursuit of bourgeois comforts at the price of conformity, the acceptance of surveillance, the delivery of culture as commodity. I seem to have thought, according to my notes, that culture was properly transferred by seduction, by the education of the senses. Under conditions of Terror, moreover, survival dictated that special attention had to be paid to fundamentals, to primitive materials, to life histories, fictions, collections.

I did write the paper, and read it one morning to a small assembly of Cuban academics, and one student, a tiny and very black girl whose face was disfigured in a childhood scalding accident, but whose eyes shone with an intense intellectual light. I saw her again over the next few days of my visit. However seemingly unplanned the encounter she each time had a question or commentary of such penetration and seriousness it could only have been developed and rehearsed over many hours. The academics who came to hear me might have had something of the comical about them were they not so similarly earnest. As compared with their students they were very white, very bourgeois, over-dressed in ill-fitting suits and ensembles with neckties and scarves, stiff in their manners and their bodies. Anti-Cuba. The opposite of the Malecón. One can only imagine the shifts and expedients that went into these types, this fiction of normal professional life.

We gathered in a small room on the upper floor of the old Havana country club, now the campus of an arts university. Outside the air was filled with tropical fragrance and the discordant sounds of young people practicing their instruments from all quarters of the campus. In the room allotted to us a noisy antique air conditioner blocked all sunlight and poured out a wet intimation of chilled meat. My heart sank well before I began reading. What did I have to say in such a place to such people that would be worth the effort they had made, the respect given on trust. Everything that was there in the paper in front of me, with its pretentious title, that I was about to say and that had to be said and would be said, because I was committed and had nothing else in reserve, now seemed foolish. But the paper had been circulated, and had obviously been read and studied, respectfully, with thoughtful questions prepared in advance. If only I had written something more pure and clean and honest and not the sort of thing one wrote for bored, indifferent, North American audiences and editors.

As it happened, the exigencies of translation into Spanish somehow redeemed everything. It sounded better in Spanish. The translator, a brisk middle-aged woman with a designer scarf at her throat, anticipated my pauses in a clear murmur of seamless, liquid antiphon. We hit our stride together at these words:

"The terror I speak of is not incompatible with a certain populism, expressed as student-centred 'choices' of programmes and courses, in commitments to universality of access, in an old-maidish concern with every sort of tender sensibility, in the general paternalism of approach to student welfare. Indeed the terror I speak of requires these manipulations in order to dilute in advance any potential formation of opposition cadres. Similarly, the emphasis on faculty career development, orderly progress through the ranks, fair and evenly applied standards for pay and promotion, has also the tendency to neutralize dissent, and also to insure that the material interests of the faculty are indistinguishable from the interests of the managerial and professional classes generally, and that this class identity is reproduced faithfully in students. It is a symptom of this populism-as-control, and not an exception to it, that the curriculum in so many arts and humanities subjects expands into domains of popular culture."

We gathered steam. It felt like a duet:

"Naturally, one may by these means have a certain local success in reproducing or simulating mastery of subject matters and so forth, but at the cost of establishing the principle of the therapeutic, the disciplinary, the instrumental, in the heart of the cultural enterprise. My point in respect of teaching culture is only that a principled response to this therapeutic regime should of all things not be itself therapeutic. It should not call attention to damaged learners, but instead to a damaged culture. This requires politicising the issue of culture at a time when politics itself is in little regard, as a practice or as a profession, and in which this de-politicising is itself mandated by the therapeutic model. Resisting the therapeutic, and the disciplinary, means a refusal to blame learners or their families. It means demanding from oneself and one's students tough analytical work on the conditions of cultural production and reproduction, with real tasks pursued to high purpose, rather than on the manipulation of factitious 'skill-sets,' the creation of 'team players,' the obsession with catching 'cheaters,' and all the rest of the terroristic programme."

From the discussion that followed, with these professors of Spanish literature, Marxist social theory, sociology of popular religious movements, none of whom made official salaries higher than those of street sweepers or bus drivers, it was clear that we really could meet, if only for a brief time, if only in the somewhat precious atmosphere of the academic meeting, on the ground of a survey of the great and general wreckage. We were brothers and sisters across the divide of our different political masters, our different compromises, our different nightmares and hopes. It was equally clear to me, gazing out over the serious and intelligent faces, that theirs was the greater dignity.

Afterwards, a tall, stooped man with narrow shoulders and prematurely grey hair and an old-fashioned and battered briefcase in his hand, invited me outside. With a few coins he purchased coffee in two small glasses from a female vendor who had set up shop on the edge of a wide veranda, whose cast iron railings had rusted, and fallen away in places, and which afforded a view of an abandoned and overgrown golf course. We chatted and sipped our tepid, bitter coffees on exactly the spot Noel Coward and Alec Guinness meet for cocktails in a scene in the 1959 Carol Reed film *Our Man in Havana*.

My Cuba notes remind me that I saw one morning an old man on his front porch doing exercises consisting of elaborate slow-motion wind-ups for imaginary baseball pitches.

    I meet in my notes another old guy with a machete, the

blade wrapped carefully in paper and string, like a Japanese parcel. His work is cutting weeds by the side of the road. We chat on a low wall at a bus stop. He is lean and scarred. He had fought in Angola. I think it must have been like this to meet one of Caesar's legionnaires, retired from the wars to Thrace, or to Cornwall. His daughter, he tells me with quiet pride, is a medical doctor, his son an engineer.

A pretty, homesick, *uruguaya* (pronounced oo-roo-gwasha she says) from Montevideo shows me how to drink maté one morning in the student hall—where I had a room and shared the evening meal with an assortment of foreign students.

The quarters were primitive. Water for showers was heated by an exposed electrical coil in each shower head, switched on by an ancient ceramic device you reached for while soaking wet. Only one of these worked anyway. A friendly rat visited regularly. The food was bland, and consisted mostly of rice and beans. Some of the students were short-term enrollees in language programs, organized from Toronto. Others were Latin American exchange students, like my lovely *uruguaya*. Yet others were vaguely described as "graduate students," Americans and Europeans who seemed to have gone native. The American and British long-term residents especially had uniformly pasty skin, something dead in the eyes, and seemed all to have research projects that were never likely to end. They were slowly becoming unfit for life anywhere else.

They were full of stories of mysterious illnesses and hair-raising rides in illegal taxis and drug-induced adventures and lapses of consciousness. And tips for survival in Castro's Cuba. Almost any likely post-Castro scenario, they agreed, would be a disaster for them personally.

I collected inscriptions.

This from a notice board for a French tour group, in the lobby of the Novotel where I went to sneak a dip in the pool:

—07:00 – douche obligatoire.

—07:30 – se brosse les dents.

Then this, low down on the tile wall of a strange, ruined Gaudiesque pavilion, a part of the Arts University, an exchange scrawled in two different hands, the first jerkily masculine, the second joined-up, feminine.

—Yo quiero amarte con todo mi amor. ¿Donde estás?

—¡Aquí! Amame, pero...¿Quién eres?

There was actually only one harlequined Venus on the Malecón, the great curving seawall and esplanade that divides Havana from the sea. An heroic, tesselated derrière under a full moon, beside the sea. She turned out to have a generous mouth, intelligent eyes, a quick smile and a flower in her hair. My companion proposed something matter-of-fact. It was received as tribute. She mentioned an hour the next day. A bus stop in a certain quarter of Havana. She darted a doubtful glance at me and mentioned a sister. My companion jotted words on a scrap of paper and folded it carefully into his wallet. But this was all chivalry, an expected courtesy. We flew out the next morning.

Prodigal Returns

The yellow school bus stopped at the end of the lane, and Eunice pushed on the big handle. She had agreed to take the strange pair out from town while she dropped off the rural kids. They had seemed harmless enough. The older of the two had said they were coming home.

"You sure it's okay to leave you here like this?" Eunice said, squinting skeptically at the deserted lane and the silent house. "I could come in and look around. Be sure your folks was here, and all."

"No, we'll be fine. Thanks for the lift," Lucy said, and stepped unsteadily in her last pair of city shoes onto the little delta of gravel and clay that spilled out the end of the lane. Eunice handed out the suitcases, and then the girl.

The two slender figures, one fair, one dark, waited by the road until they heard Eunice double declutch into third, and saw her disappear over the hill.

Lucy looked at the tall grass and the Queen-Anne's lace,

the chicory, the bed-straws and sweet clover, waist high in the shallow ditch. She sniffed the air and straightened her back. She handed the girl her suitcase and picked up her own and walked up the lane.

The house and farm were neglected. A corner of the porch needed propping up and the lattice-work below was missing slats. There were no sheep in the meadow beyond the drive shed, and the corn crib was empty. Less than half of the big kitchen garden had been cultivated. Portulaca ran freely in the rows. Pig-weed and burdock had taken over the abandoned portions.

In the summer kitchen the walls were streaked with soot, dead flies lay thick on the sills, the cupboard doors were stained and greasy. Empty canning jars sat on an oil-cloth-covered table. Bunches of dusty herbs from other years hung from the ceiling. A string above the stove was festooned with drying dish cloths. A pot bubbled on the back lid.

Lucy seemed to know her way around. She shook down the ash with an expert twist, tipped up the front lid with the lifter, and put a billet of wood on the fire from the small woodbox at the side.

Lucy turned to the girl. "What you think?"

Jacky touched the hot stove experimentally. She was thin and round-shouldered and had sharp features, black hair and eyes, and faded acne scars on her cheeks. She said nothing.

Behind the kitchen door Lucy found straw hats and a pair of rubber boots. Under a bench by the window she found another pair. They put these things on and went out into the yard.

The drive-shed turned up one good hoe and one with half the blade broke off. They began attacking the portulaca between the rows of beans. Lucy showed Jacky how to come down hard with the corner of the hoe, raising a clod, then chopping the clod fine, and smoothing it all out with the blade, teasing the weeds to the surface and pushing them into little piles to die exposed in the sun.

They had half a row done, after a fashion, flailing away, and grinning at one another, when Jacky's eyes rolled back in her head and she fainted in a heap on the ground.

Before she could get to the girl, Lucy heard the screen door and turned to see Mrs. Brubacher, blinking in the sunlight, her prayer-cap askew. She had been sleeping under the stairs, as she used to do. "Help me get her in," Lucy called out. "She's not so good."

Mrs. Brubacher disappeared back through the screen door. In an instant it exploded open again and Mrs. Brubacher emerged with a big black umbrella, a wet cloth and a pillow. She moved over the grass with heavy efficiency, opening the umbrella as she came, and handed it to Lucy to hold over the girl. She put the pillow under the girl's head and knelt down and wiped her face and throat and wrists gently with the wet cloth, and blew on her to cool her down, and wiped a bit more, and blew, until the girl's eyes fluttered.

Only when Jacky got some colour in her lips and eyelids, and smiled weakly at them, would Mrs. Brubacher permit them to move her, which they did with exaggerated care, carrying the girl between them in a chair made of their locked arms.

Jacky dozed on the flop-bench in the corner. Lucy and Mrs. Brubacher made pot pie. Under the gentle kerosene hiss of the Aladdin lamp they rolled out the dough, and peeled carrots and potatoes and cut up the chicken to boil. Mrs. Brubacher said she had always wanted to go to the Holy Land, and guessed she never would. The blueberries was small this year, but real tasty. They said nothing to one another about Lucy's sudden and unexpected return. Lucy gathered that Mr. Brubacher had been dead for a long time. She frequently touched Mrs. Brubacher's arm as they worked, and got her a stool, and fetched water from the pump for her, and in those moments Mrs. Brubacher looked searchingly at Lucy with round innocent eyes and the corners of her mouth briefly trembled.

In the weeks that followed, Lucy made inventories of things that needed doing around the house and farm. She found old work clothes of Mr. Brubacher's, and assembled what she could of tools and paint brushes, and found a cache of forgotten paint cans, some full and some half-full, and rags and nails and such things. She repaired the porch and painted it. She sanded all the surfaces in the outhouse in the bottom of the yard until the seat was like velvet and the place smelt of pine. She worked in the garden in the evening when the sun was low. She thought of acquiring some sheep in the spring.

Lucy became strong, and ate with gusto. Her hands toughened from the work and turned brown in the sun. She looked with pleasure on her new body when she sat in the tin tub in the evening by the stove. Returning strength and the blessing of work also brought to her mind a flood of grief and humility. She let these feelings have full play, and went alone to her old favourite places and wept and argued with herself.

In a drawer in her room Lucy found some of her old dresses—which, in her new lean condition, fitted her perfectly—and prayer caps, and black cotton stockings, and in a cupboard a pair of plain black shoes. She took to wearing these on Sundays when they sat around the table, and then began wearing them during the week. Mrs. Brubacher made some more dresses for Lucy from the old patterns, and for Jacky too. Lucy and Jacky brushed each other's hair in the evening under the Aladdin, and in the morning arranged it for the day, drawn up under the cap and a little bit showing at the front with a part in the middle.

Jacky found Mr. Brubacher's old single-shot .22 and a box of shorts. She cleaned the rifle with Mrs. Brubacher's sewing machine oil and rags and a bit of worn-out steel wool, and made the rifle gleam, and hung it on the wall, and shot pigeons for their supper. She sat in the big lawn chair with the fan-shaped back and picked them off the tin roof of the drive-shed.

But Jacky had no stamina for the jobs Lucy did. She got tired quickly and her lips and eyelids were always white.

Jacky and Lucy slept together in the upstairs bedroom that had been the Brubachers'. Mrs. Brubacher now only slept under the stairs, and often wandered about in the night, and talked to herself. Sometimes, lying awake, listening for Mrs. Brubacher to settle down, Lucy tried to will strength from herself into Jacky's body. She took her in her arms and blew softly on her neck and held Jacky's little shoulder blades against her breasts and Jacky's thin buttocks against her belly, and felt helpless, and was tempted to despair.

In the day they were busy and the work went well. Autumn was approaching and the crisp air invigorated them. They gathered apples from the overgrown orchard.

Mrs. Brubacher put up beans and made apple butter, and while she worked, Jacky told her about her life in the city. Mrs. Brubacher could make nothing of this, and perhaps supposed she was listening to stories from the mission field. She would say "Lan' sakes," or "Don't that beat all," and open her eyes wide. When Mrs. Brubacher lay down for her naps under the stairs Jacky took off Mrs. Brubacher's prayer cap and shoes and put something over her.

About the beginning of October Jacky got much worse. She had trouble getting out of bed in the morning, and she was never warm enough. She sat by the stove in the kitchen, so close her shins broke out in red marks. Then she couldn't do anything at all, and wouldn't eat, and slept most of the day on the flop-bench in the kitchen. At night Lucy held her closer than ever, and put an extra blanket on them until she was covered in sweat herself. But it did no good; Jacky came down with fever, and one night had convulsions.

The next morning Lucy walked to the nearest farm with a telephone and called a doctor.

He was a long time with Jacky, in their bedroom, where Lucy had carried her and put her in the middle of the big bed.

When the doctor came down, and had washed his hands in a basin of warm water Lucy had set on the table, and dried his hands on the towel she had put there for him, he turned to Lucy and said, "She's very sick."

"Can you do anything for her?" Lucy asked.

The doctor was a large and florid man of sixty. He looked shrewdly at Lucy. Her voice was beautiful. Not the voice of a local woman. And the girl was not from here either.

"Your sister?" he asked, more gruffly than he intended.

Lucy didn't answer.

The doctor looked around at Mrs. Brubacher, who stood near the door, her prayer cap slightly askew and a strand of grey hair hanging down over her face, her eyes round and childlike.

"No," he said, "there's not much I can do. She's anaemic of course. I took a blood sample to be analyzed, but I think she has a disease of the red blood cells. Pernicious anaemia. Do you know what that means?"

"Yes," Lucy said.

"Keep her warm. Get her to drink water."

He hesitated, considering how much he should say.

"In her condition an infection is especially dangerous. She may contract pneumonia." He paused. "That would be perhaps merciful."

He put on his coat and took his hat from Lucy. He glanced at Mrs. Brubacher and said quietly to Lucy, "Would you follow me to the car?"

Lucy threw a coat around her shoulders, and put a black bonnet over her prayer cap. She wore these things all the time now.

The light outside was just going. It was cold but very still. The mist of their breaths hung before them like words that cannot be taken back.

"Miss Brubacher."

Lucy looked up, startled. She had not heard herself called that in many years.

"I will look in again."

There was something else. The doctor looked away for a moment, and then directly at Lucy. He could see in her eyes that she didn't know.

"Your sister is pregnant."

Lucy felt a heavy weight in her chest growing and pulling downward. She could scarcely bear it.

"How far?" Lucy asked in a whisper.

"Four, five months. Maybe more. I doubt the baby is developing very well."

The doctor put on his hat and got into his car. He watched Lucy for a moment, standing alone and still in the cold air. He started the car and backed up to the drive shed, shifted into first and drove slowly out the lane.

Jacky lasted two more weeks. She died quietly on the day of the first snow. Lucy shut Jacky's eyes and washed her body and wrapped it in the best sheet they had, and made up a trestle for the coffin in the parlour they never went into, next to the fancy parlour-stove, now cold, that looked like a church, with the books all around that had comforted and transported Lucy as a child, the foundling Lucy alone in an immense sea, the little Crusoe ship-wrecked again.

In the orchard, after she had done what she needed to do,

and the undertaker had come and gone for the last time, Lucy tried vainly to enlist the trees in her cause, running from one to another and hitting them, unreasonably, with her strong brown hands, until she exhausted herself, and lay down weeping amid the great fruit-bearing matriarchs, among the fragrant windfall apples, each with its own fairy-cap of snow, and let the snow cover her too.

Before the end of winter Mrs. Brubacher's times grew so bad she one day attacked Lucy with a shovel and had to be put in a home. Lucy sold the farm to pay for Mrs. Brubacher's keep, and moved back to the city.

Prodigal Returns appeared shortly after, a first collection that announced with raw authority the themes that would continue to occupy Lucy Brubacher's best, most mature poems—themes of betrayal, disappointment, loss, redemption. The front of the dust-jacket bore a photo, an old snapshot taken slightly askew, a girl in the lower right portion of the picture, in a pinafore, a young-old face under a dark bonnet, running it seems toward the camera. The rest of the picture shows the corner of a shed or barn, some hens, a dark figure seen only from the waist down, a man, his hand holding some agricultural implement, perhaps a flail.

The Walk

On the last day of M.'s life he takes a walk around the lake, as he has many times before. Being in no hurry and anyway feeling a certain heaviness in his limbs—a hint of vertigo and shortness of breath, not in themselves distressing or even unpleasant, sensations he attributes to the warmth and humidity of the day—he lingers by the war memorial.

The monument stands on a walled parapet. On a stone plinth are two lifesize bronze figures, the first bareheaded and exultant, the second hooded and bowed. Bronze plaques display names of the dead. Broad steps descend in front toward the lake.

M. seats himself on a corner of the wall at the top of the steps, from where he can if he wishes gaze out over the lake and the expanse of lawn below, while keeping in view the two bronze figures of the monument, figures which now seem to him, by a slow percolation of awareness, neither redundant nor conventional but hinting obscurely at narrative.

The lawn is peopled sparsely with strollers and their dogs and children, and solitary figures sitting or lying. The scene swims before his eyes in a pointillist shimmer and the strollers and dogs and children freeze momentarily and then resume their movements.

He notices a woman, sitting alone at a wooden picnic table, perched sideways on the bench, her back to him, leaning on her left elbow. Her right leg extends out to her side, her naked foot tensed as though for the start of a race or some other sudden springing movement. Shining black hair, a black dress of clinging jersey negligently disposed, ruched carelessly high up on her thigh. Her leg is massy in all its parts, the strong masculine knee, the muscular thigh and calf, the roughly-modeled squarish anklebone, the prominent Achilles' tendon, the burnished crook of the heel.

M. looks again at the bronze figures. The downcast hooded figure, the one closest to him, a broken sword at its side, its gown, or shroud, parted to reveal a naked leg arrested in mid-stride, a sense neither of motion nor of rest, but of strained immobility, a frozen energy amounting to a moral idea. This foot, more particularly the heel, like the woman's a noble bulb or rootstock supported in a bridgework of tendons and the massive arch of the instep.

The seed of the woman shall crush the serpent under his heel. Is this inscribed on the monument? M. thinks it must be. He moves from his perch on the wall and circles the figures on the war memorial. He cannot find it. It is from the Bible.

M. returns to the head of the steps and looks out again over the lawn and the lake. The woman in black is no longer at the picnic table. A middle-aged couple are sitting there instead. A chequered cloth covers the table and on it, the remains of a breakfast. They have evidently been there for a long time.

Then he sees her. The high waist and the outline of powerful legs, in black, standing in the path beyond the band shell. Although far away, she is now level with him and this circumstance heightens the impression of connection, a certainty that she is looking at him, communing with him.

She wants him to look across the lake. He does not know how he knows this. There is no longer just the two of them, but a third, across the lake, making a triangle. The atmosphere vibrates with this knowledge, as though a chord has been struck at oscillations inaudible to the human ear but registering in a deep layer of the mind and will. He finds himself looking directly at a spot framed by elder bushes growing at the water's edge on the far side of the lake, at the foot of a lawn and garden sweeping up to a large house with white columns and a tall blue spruce and a tennis court. A youth stands there, androgynous, slender, fair, round-shouldered and tentative, looking directly at him.

M. has moved further around the shore of the lake. The sun

slants from the southeast, low through the willow branches. By the side of the path a little busker whom M. takes at first for a child. The body of a thirteen-year old, a broad, blonde, freckled face with no eyelashes or any particular colour in the eyes. Long strawberry hair, clean, but curiously lifeless, straw-like.

M. now sees that the face is an old face, ancient, blind. She wears a blue-black velvet dress, an ill-fitting cast-off theatrical costume, a long dress, its frogging or buttons or other ornaments missing, torn away, her bare feet visible below the dragging hem, a single gold ring on one of her toes. She plays a small violin, a child's version with a thin, reedy tone, with surprising vigour, a tune M. thinks he should know. From childhood, a chipped 78 spinning under a steel needle. The little busker's instrument case is open on the pavement at her feet and the bottom is covered with large dull yellow coins and a sprinkling of silver, all strange and foreign. M. recognizes the tune, a humoresque, which has begun again without a break. He can't recall the composer.

People, tourists mostly, stroll here and there in twos and threes. Rather too randomly, he thinks, like extras hired for a promotion, to give the appearance of naturalness without quite succeeding. They seem oblivious to the busker, perhaps do not see her or hear her. Ahead somewhere her familiar, her controller, the dark woman of the heel, waiting, drawing this procession to its predestined end. And across the lake, hidden now, but listening also, without doubt, to the fantastic strains of the violin, the slender youth,

M. feels in this a certain impatience, and even anger. The anger is invigorating. These hallucinations—what else could they be?—but no, not so slight a thing, psychologically, as hallucinations, but rather symbols, no, not so much as that. Conceits—of a tiresomely literary type.

It comes, as it must, sooner or later, the memory of another day, another place. Thirty years past. Not far from here. High, exposed fields, a height-of-land, a watershed, sloping away to east and west, pitched finely to the south. Only a barn left standing of all the old farm buildings. Two or three leaning hollowed-out apple trees, the vestiges of an orchard. A weed-filled lane. Fragments of a rail fence like the dots and dashes of a code. In the tall grass near the barn, a well. Perhaps it is there yet. Still partly covered with rotting boards.

M. has passed the spot frequently but never stops, the farm being anyway, on a half-hour of back roads, only one of many stations, as in a pilgrimage. Three crossroads, five churches, one river, one wet wood of ghostly deer and fetid mists, reversible in order, east to west or west to east.

A wind blows over the lake, the farther shore recedes, waves begin to break at M.'s feet as on an ocean shore. A ferry appears, a longboat, with a lone occupant, an oarsman. M. steps firmly aboard. "Will he be there? On the other side?"

M. asks. The ferryman says nothing. M. sees that the face of the ferryman is the face of his father, but younger, younger than M. is now, and the face wears an expression of remote detachment and amusement. As the boat speeds away into the waves, the ferryman says, "Let us all stand up," as though repeating the punchline of an ancient joke whose meaning is lost.

Afterword

The stories collected here were written over a period of about twenty years. Most have appeared in whole or in part in literary magazines or in anthologies edited by others. Only one is entirely new. Some are pure fictions. Some scarcely bother to conceal their character as memoir. Yet others are somewhere in between: stories that have a basis in experience but took their own way from the start. Settings and situations of course reflect passages of my history, most of which need no explanation. The strangest of them to many readers will be the world of Norwegian immigrant chapel-folk in New York City, into which I was born. This was the setting of *Sister Patsy*, my first novel, and of parts of *The Yellow Room*. The novella that opens this collection, while mostly about something else entirely, is linked to that world in a significant way, and may be regarded as the final part of a Sunset Park trilogy. Many of the stories draw from this same well.

Two themes or devices recur frequently in these stories. The first, not surprisingly, is the attraction of men and women to one another, in all its urgent, baffling mystery. The other is the disruptive authority of an image: perhaps a photograph, or the involuntary stirring of a memory. If sexual attraction is often the motive force in these tales, it is the resurrection of some frozen particle of time that as often arrests or diverts the course of events—or the attention of the narrator—changing the story itself into something utterly different and strange.

I was not aware in writing these stories of an intention to set out these themes; I must suppose they stem from a deep personal source. Or perhaps these are the inevitable themes of a certain kind of writing in a certain kind of era. The narrator of the story of the Venus on the Malecón believes that a Time of Terror calls for the most elementary of reconstructions: "primitive materials . . . life histories, fictions, collections."